The Stolen Child

The Stolen Child

A Novel
by
PAUL CODY

BASKERVILLE
PUBLISHERS, INC.
DALLAS • NEW YORK • DUBLIN

BASKERVILLE Publishers, Inc.
7616 LBJ Freeway, Suite 220, Dallas, TX 75251-1008

Library of Congress Cataloging-in-Publication Data

Cody, Paul, 1953-
    The stolen child : a novel / by Paul Cody.
        p.   cm.
    ISBN 1-880909-30-8
    I. Title.
PS3553.0335S76 1995
813 '.54--dc20
                                                        94-45384
                                                              CIP

Manufactured in the United States of America
First Printing, 1995

For Liz and Liam

Come away, O human child!
To the waters and the wild

                              —W.B. Yeats

[1]   Medfield State Hospital

He disappeared on a Friday afternoon in October. He was nine or ten years old, and he may have been riding a bicycle, or he may have been walking. The day was warm, the leaves were orange and red and gold, and he was probably alone—somewhere in Newton, outside Boston. He was wearing jeans and a baseball cap and sneakers, and maybe he was on Walnut Street, near Newtonville Square, and a car pulled up. A blue car, a red car, a car with out-of-state plates, and the driver rolled down the window, and said, Hey, said, Hello, asked for directions, wanted to know the time. You want a lift? the driver may have asked, and Ford stopped, turned, smiled. He had freckles, straight brown hair, blue eyes.

This was a long time ago, and he might be someplace now, might be in some town or city, some state or country or continent. He'd be older, and he could have a new family, a family of his own, or maybe just a room to himself.

Or he might be dead. Probably he's dead. He could have drowned, could have been shot or strangled or stabbed or smothered, and left somewhere. In woods, in a dumpster, at the edge of a lake. Maybe his body was found in the Utah desert, or in a motel room, off an interstate, in Missouri or Nevada or Florida. There were blinking neon lights, anemic palm trees, the whine of traffic in the distance. An insect ticking against a window.

Other things are possible too. Everything's possible.

Ford went to live in a castle, in a country beyond a sea somewhere. He had a room at the top of a winding stair, with a bed as wide as a pond. At night there were blinking lights outside the window next to his bed, a mile or two away.

This is Ireland, he thought. This is Kenya. This is India. This is the western part of Canada.

The few people he saw never spoke. They seemed to drift and float, and they brought food to him on trays, and drew baths, and smiled at him like this was a kingdom somewhere in Mexico, or this was Heaven, and God was very tired, was sleeping, in a far high room of the castle. He'd sleep a long time. Would sleep for a month or a year, or he would sleep an hour or two more, and then send a helper in a crimson robe to Ford, and the helper—an old woman with a kind face—would gesture with her pale hand, would move as though to say, Come with me. Come along, and she'd turn, would begin to glide away, down a long long corridor.

Ford would follow. He'd think, This is not Canada. This is not India or Ireland. This is on the way to God, and he'd want to cry and run past the robed woman, and he'd want to turn, because to see God in his castle was to be dead, and he'd turn to the side and there were carved doors with keys in their locks, and he would be ten years old, and this started in Newtonville Square, and Mom told him to be careful. The car paused, and the man smiled like a baseball coach, a priest, like a fourth-grade teacher. And now God was waiting, was lying awake in bed, his eyes dark and liquid, and the room was full of mist.

So there's nothing tonight. Nothing now or any night.

Not in the doors or walls, not in the locks, not in the floor, the ceiling, the bars on the windows. Just breathing slow and waiting, and at ten the attendants will come through with their keys and long policeman's flashlights, and if anyone lingers in the halls or dayroom, they'll say, Okay. Let's go. It's time, they'll say, their voices as quiet and still as darkness.

The beams of light will move fast over the walls and ceiling, and voices whisper and mutter, say, No, no, no, no, and I don't move or say anything or even think to breathe. I'm quiet and patient as dust.

Footsteps shuffle past, slippers pad the linoleum, and the feet go quick, then slow, and the voices whisper, Sorry, okay, and sorry, okay, and a steel door clanks somewhere, goes boom, and keys jangle like music, and more shuffling footsteps go by. They squeak. They're sneakers.

Then they'll say, Okay, it's time, and I'll shuffle along too, and I'll nod and smile, and they won't even have to tell me to roll up the sleeve of my tee shirt. They'll touch the spot with cotton, and it's ice for a second, then the needle will be so fast I won't realize till afterward that they're done. That the chemical's inside, and spreading through me, and it could last a long time if it had to, could last until after I'm out and in a room with a hotplate. With a bulb in the ceiling. A wire running along the bottom of the wall.

All set, the man in white will say, and I'll nod some more.

Then it's getting dark. The lawns outside are deep deep green, and full of shadow, and a bird clicks in a tree, goes click, click, cheep, click, and I walk slowly in the light that's being covered over with shadows outside. And there are shadows in here too. Night with its blankets of darkness, and more men go past with keys, and the one with black hair says, Ellis, as I shuffle past, and I don't say anything.

Some patients have bathrobes and pajama bottoms that are too big, and white tee shirts with Luckies or Marlboros in the sleeve. But no matches or lighters. The attendants have those.

Walter does, and Rick, and John.

You bend over with the cigarette in your mouth, and they flick their hand, their lighters, and your face glows, then a big cloud, then thanks, then okay. No problem.

And along and slow I go, and the chemical's spreading inside deeper and deeper. I'm slow as syrup. I won't pour in here.

The wall's half green and half tan, and cool as November, even though the leaves are just beginning to fall on the long lawns. Lawns that are now falling with shadow.

My face is against the wall, and I press my hands down. One on the wall, one on my side, at the hip.

Rick says, Ellis, and I smile, and he puts his hand on my shoulder blade in back, and I'm fine as Friday or Saturday.

The wall is cool against my cheek.

The dayroom's dark except for the flickering gray light of television. No sound, just flickering, and red EXIT signs over the door, even though it's locked, and Rick or John would have to let us out.

I sit near the window, near the television. Flicker and flicker, and outside there's the lawn in back, and beyond that another building with pale lights in windows, and the sky's getting grayer and quieter and almost black. Leaves are whisking in branches. Leaves dry like paper, and some are on the ground already.

Okay, they say, and Marshall's near another window, looking out, and his fingers move all the time, going fret and fret. His fingers are knitting needles or birds going click click click, faster and faster. Always the fingers go-

4

ing and going.

John comes in and says, Okay. He says, Marshall, and Marshall stands by the window, his hands still going, his head down, and John goes over and touches his arm.

Almost time, John says.

Marshall, he says. Almost nine-thirty, and touches Marshall's arm and shoulder, and the hands go and go, and then Marshall turns and moves fast away from the window, and outside a car with headlights like cat eyes moves between two buildings, past lawns that are black. Then red eyes behind. First white and yellow, then red like candy.

Don't say that, Marshall whispers, then he's gone, and John has a policeman's flashlight, and squeaking sneakers.

Ellis, he says. It's almost ten, you know, and he's gone, and it's flickering light and no sound. It's the window, and chairs, and the table the television's bolted to, and I'm in here too, and I'm slow as stone now. I'm dumb as a bag of dimes. Slow and dense, and the chemical's all the way through me, and someone's calling, Get ready, then whispery voices say things I can't make out.

I don't say anything, and this is twenty miles from Boston, Massachusetts maybe. Plymouth Rock and beans and the Mayflower.

Ellis, Walter says, and it's no whisper.

Let's go, pal, he tells me, and his keys jangle, and his feet squeak.

I don't wanna have to tell you again.

My feet are white, and my toes long, and the linoleum has speckles.

Look at me, Ellis, and his beard is blond, and he says, We're almost at ten. You know the rules.

About moving slow, and going for a long time. The windows are dark squares now, and everyone's gone except for John and Walter and Rick, and they're slow too. They don't move as fast.

There's a long row of doors, and breathing behind every one of them.

The sheets are cool, and have old yellow stains, and there's a wardrobe at the foot of the bed, with two hangers, and the red sweater they let me borrow, and a window, and outside the lawn, and past the lawn some woods. And things in the woods. Trees, and bushes, and maybe a man squatting and watching, his eyes glittery in the dark. Waiting for hour after hour, his eyes blinking, and he's barely breathing at all.

My head is heavy on the pillow. It must weigh ten or twenty pounds. And all the wires inside. The blips, the tiny sparks, like atoms in deep space, flicking and flicking.

Footsteps in the hall. Shuffling, then the ceiling way up there, and a piece of light in a corner, a tan square pasted in place. If I wake up in an hour the square will be different, because they snuck in and moved it.

And the man's sitting in the woods out there. Quiet like a tree or leaf. His eyes shining, and watching for hour after hour.

The man has a car, and he can move if he wants. Can drive all night and the next day and that night as well. Can go forty or fifty hours, and pull over once or twice in a rest stop, under trees, near overflowing trash cans. He can slump down behind the wheel and close his eyes, and feel the engine still vibrating, and the road underneath, even though everything has stopped.

The light falls on his eyelids, outside Albany, New York or Jackson, Mississippi.

He can drift like that. His eyes closed, and the sounds of the road seem a long long way away. Maybe there's a sound from beyond the trees too. A branch or a squirrel.

Rustling. And the man's somewhere along there, and drifting like a leaf on water, and a car comes through, passes slowly, then stops ten or twenty feet beyond. The car doors—one, then a second—open and close, and the sound is way far off.

Drifting like in here. My head a hundred pounds, and full of old coins that have been in the attic or something. Musty coins. Maybe they were under water.

And the man could sit, his eyes still closed, only he hears footsteps, and the click of a dog's collar and leash.

The girl at the rest stop is maybe ten, and wearing yellow shorts, and a tee shirt with birds on it that has to be two or three sizes too big. She's wearing sneakers, and ankle socks, and the dog's a beagle, probably just a puppy. The girl has short dark hair, and a cloth bracelet on one thin wrist.

The dog pauses and sniffs, and she pauses with him, and her arms are bare like the branches of a sapling.

The man is in the car—his eyes are mostly closed, and he can see a reddish tint from the blood in his eyelids, and he moves his head slightly.

She looks over, he smiles.

The girl's mother comes out of the women's part of the cinderblock restrooms.

Andrea, the mother says, and the girl turns, and his eyes are closed, and he's been awake for thirty-six hours, and he started in Maryland Wednesday morning.

It's Thursday, the radio said, so he left Wednesday, near Virginia and the shore, and the place near the bar. It had a neon palm tree, and a mounted deer head over the door.

He's a man near Albany, and he's been driving so long he can't remember when he started.

There was a hitchhiker in New Jersey who wore a suede vest, and the hitchhiker wanted to get to Edison.

Rick leans in with his flashlight. There's a spot on the

ceiling.

Ellis, he says. Can't sleep?

My head goes from side to side.

Another half hour or hour, you let us know. We'll get you a shot.

Sleep is what happens at the end of a day. It comes up to you, quiet and soft, and you don't even know it.

Ford walked with his mother in a park in Newton, and the baby was in a baby carriage, and the baby's name was James, and he was Ford's brother. Ford would grow up and love him very much and watch over him. Ford was the only brother James would ever have, Mom said.

She was happy because spring had finally arrived, and the leaves were beginning to come out on the trees, and there were flowers in bloom. Red flowers and yellow and white flowers. Sometimes, she said, it seemed like spring would never arrive, and that the snow and ice were there to stay forever. But then the sun grew warm, and she almost felt like she would sing, she was so happy.

A man in a suit and tie walked by. He was bald and his head was shiny like the top of a car. He nodded and smiled at them. He said, Lovely day, and Mom said, Yes, it is.

There was another big man in Missouri or Oregon. In North Dakota or Michigan—near the Canadian border. Driving slow in the morning, in the school zone. There was an old man, a crossing guard, parked near the intersection, wearing an orange vest, holding a portable STOP sign. Kids came by, and the man driving, the big man, went slow, then stopped, and waved to the old man.

Two kids passed, then four more. They were all in sneakers, carrying lunch satchels and small backpacks. One had his shoestrings flapping and dangling, his shirttails out, and it was barely eight in the morning.

The kids passed, and the old man, the crossing guard,

his face brown, his stomach sagging, lowered the sign and shuffled to his car at the side of the intersection.

At night in Boston, I drove along Commonwealth Avenue, and very late, long after midnight, I moved slowly toward the bus station, and the kids were out front, on the sidewalk—skinny kids, with dirty hair, and jean jackets, and tee shirts, and no socks.

A girl came to the car window and said, Hey, said, What're you doing.

You wanna fuck me, she said, and behind her a kid with a cap on backwards said, You can fuck my girlfriend, you want, or you can fuck me.

The wall is smooth and cool, and here in October, the leaves are quiet when they fall. It's maybe eleven by now, and I could get up and say, I can't sleep. I can never sleep. I lie there hour after hour.

Like the man in the woods, squatting, or the man near Albany, or me at the bus station, and the girl and the boy at my car window, and two or three others crowding behind.

Where you from? I asked, and one of them said, Russia, and another said, The moon, then they laughed, and said, Where you from?

I get up and the bedsprings squeak, and I sit on the side of my bed. The blanket itches.

Outside it's darker still, and the tops of trees are humps, and the sky is moonless and starless. It's maybe eleven. No more. Rick and Walter and John are gone. And only Steve's out in the halls after eleven. The shift supervisor comes by every two or three hours. Steve goes to school days, and weighs two hundred and fifty pounds, and reads all night.

The window has bars on the outside, and water is dripping in a pipe. Water sloshes and slaps, and the man in the woods is somewhere.

Tate, from long ago, would know about him and where he came from. Tate would lean over and whisper, I'm crazy about you.

She'd come in and ask if she could bring me an icepack for my head.

She had light hair, and thin legs, and she squinted, but it was from habit or nerves, not her eyes.

Tell me where you go, Tate said. Tell me where you been.

She read about sun signs and earth signs. She read about ancient people who lived in South America, and who may have had giant landing strips for their space vehicles.

It's crazy, she said. I know that. But how do you explain these marks on the stones. They couldn't have done that. You could only see that from the sky.

Her eyes were brown, and she wore a tee shirt and nothing else, and she had to get up for work in only three more hours.

Then I was in a rented room. I'd been there two or three weeks, and the walls were wet, and I thought I was near Boston, was near a power plant and a canal, and there was a rip in the shade. Every day was eighty or ninety and humid, and a radio played somewhere, and late at night there were voices in the street, and bells ringing, and a bottle smashed.

I ate Saltines, and hot dogs I boiled in a pan on the hotplate, and there was a store downstairs and two doors over.

People watched me in the store, and I forgot to wear underwear. Tate was somewhere else. Tate was earlier. Maybe in Pennsylvania or Texas or Florida. There were miles and miles of road and poles, and wire strung from pole to pole. There were twangs.

But in the room I was quiet, and only went out to the

store for crackers and wine, and someone banged on the door, again and again, waited, banged again, and I didn't breathe.

I didn't know who was behind the door. On either side even.

Day after day I stayed there, and noise came from the hall. A baby crying, and doors banging, and once it rained very late at night. It sounded at first like wind, and leaves rustling, but was a wet sound, was pattering against the screen in the window.

I was in Florida, under palm trees, and I parked my car at midnight, in the neighborhood with big houses, with the water just a hundred feet away. The boats were at their moorings, silent and white in the moonlight. And big houses, with screened porches, and two or three cars, lawn furniture, high bushes between the yards.

I sat behind a house that must have had a half acre of lawn, and an apartment over the garage where the help lived. There was a light in two windows to the right, and there were shadows on the shade, and wind chimes on the screened porch.

I got up from the lawn chair, and moved closer to the bushes and house, and there was a man behind the shade. Wide shoulders, a belly, short hair.

Then a woman, lifting something, a sweater or jersey over her head, and a light went out, and there was a lower, dimmer light, then no movement, no shadows.

The wind chimes pinged, and I sat on the grass again, and lay back, and the stars were up there in the sky. The grass was cool, and then there was no light in the two windows.

I must have fallen asleep, because when I woke up it seemed like three or four a.m., and darker and quieter. A rope slapped a pole on one of the boats, and I saw stars.

Then I stood up and moved through the bushes, into

another yard. The house was two stories tall and completely dark, and I went close to the house. There was rhododendron and something that smelled like oranges, and the ground was soft. My feet sank an inch or two.

I tried the screen on the window, but it wouldn't move. I put my face close to the screen, but all I could see was darkness. I went around to the side, and tried the door to the screen porch. It was open, and I went in.

There was a glass table, and a chaise longue and two chairs. I sat down in one chair, then tried the chaise longue.

How long till the occupants, till the police, till some man comes, I wondered.

Then I was in the rented room near Boston, and the police were standing next to my bed. One of them was only twenty-two or-three, and the other was very big. They wore dark blue uniforms, and had guns and keys, handcuffs, radios.

They said, Okay, pal.

They said, What's your name? What're you doing? How long you been here?

They said, Maybe you should take a ride with us. Maybe we can find you some help.

The lights were bright, and there were speakers, and names being called.

This was not Florida or California. Not Texas or Oregon or Pennsylvania.

Tate was gone, and when they rubbed the spot on my upper arm, it was me and not someone else. And Ford became Ellis, became Ellis, became Ellis.

I knew that, and I knew about a long time ago, and what a man might have said to Ford.

How he was on his bicycle, and he was near Newtonville Square, and a car pulled up. This was Friday, and this was a long long time ago. The leaves were as bright as small suns. Orange and yellow, red like tulips.

The man rolled down the window and smiled. He said, I'm not from around here, and I'm kind of lost.

A nice bright boy like you.

The light moves down the hall, on the ceiling and walls, and Steve says, Ellis, and I stand up, and he puts his hand on my shoulder, on my upper arm, where the shot will go.

And Steve hardly says a word.

There are fifty states, and ten million miles of roads, and houses and schools, churches, playgrounds, gas stations and stores.

The car had a low hum, and I could drive forever. I could go for two or three or four days. I had small triangular tablets. I bought them at the truckstops. Twenty hits of speed for ten dollars, and I was never hungry. I sipped beer to take down the broken edges. Beer and sandpaper.

Mom said, Watch out. Be careful.

And all those faces on the sides of milk cartons, on the bulletin boards in laundromats and supermarkets. The clean hair, the large eyes. Gone from Eugene, Oregon and Melbourne, Florida. From Dandridge, Tennessee and Newton, Massachusetts.

Kids wearing blue sneakers, white jeans, a jersey with red stripes. Wearing a green parka, a checked shirt, boat shoes, boots. Wearing a New York Yankees baseball cap, a yellow windbreaker. With braces, a crescent scar on the left forearm, brown hair, green eyes. Weighing sixty-five pounds, eighty-three, fifty pounds. Four feet, six inches tall, four one, four feet, ten inches. Born in 1953, 1969, 1988.

Last seen on a playground, at a mall, on the way home from a neighbor's house.

There's been a terrible accident. We're going to your aunt's house.

Your mother had to go away. There was an emergency. She wanted you to come with me.

Shut your fucking mouth or you're dead.

I won't hurt you.

You're safe.

I'm a nightmare, he said, his voice a slap.

She'll call in a few weeks.

And on the floor in the back of the car the carpet smelled of beer and urine and gasoline, and he drove forever and ever. It was light, then dark, then light again. In Ohio or Missouri, or Arizona. There was cactus out the window. Cows, hills and farms, mountains, desert.

There was a motel room where the water dripped in the shower, and the man snored when he slept, and neon blinked Vacancy Vacancy Vacancy all through the night.

My head is a thousand pounds, and my body is light. Five or six days and nights since the police brought me here from the rented room.

Mom said, Honey, and she rubbed the towel in my hair. She said at night the world was big like the sky. She said she'd take me places. When she was a girl, her father and mother took her to a lake one summer, and there were loons and deer, raccoons and bluebirds.

She sat on the edge of the bed and said, Having you was the happiest thing in the world. She smelled like lilac, and it was October, and I was not dreaming.

[2] Ellen

This was a long time ago. Something like twenty-five or thirty years, I'm afraid to say, but I can remember it like it was last week or last night or two hours ago. Maybe because I had two young ones of my own back then—younger than he was at the time. They were home with Bernard, before Bernie and I split up, and long before I met Allen and everything changed.

Bernie was out of work as usual, probably with his back and such, and he looked after Ted and Theresa in the evenings. And I have to credit him where Ted and Theresa are concerned. He cooked them a nice hot meal—meatloaf and macaroni and cheese, peas, carrots, creamed corn, and he even made salads and made them drink their milk. And he was very good with seeing they took their baths and brushed their teeth. And later Terri told me he even read to them from one of their picture books, though he never said anything to me about that, and the two of them—Terri and Ted—never said a word.

I'm sorry in a way I didn't know about that, about Bernard reading to them. It wouldn't have made any difference, but maybe it would have too.

I didn't believe it later, when Terri told me. I kept trying to picture Bernie in his flannel shirt and the blue work pants and boots. Wearing those glasses with the black frames, and not having shaved so his face looked almost blue around the mouth and neck. Bernie at the side of the bed reading about ducks or bears or the Chinese boy who swallowed the sea.

As I said I didn't believe it when Terri told me, then I asked and Ted said sure, he read to them all the time, always sitting on the side of the bed, and reading for as long as they wanted. One more, Dad, I pictured them saying. Please, Dad. Don't stop. And Bernie not saying much. Turning a page, and finding one with a prince and a magic carpet, or the woodsman and the lady.

Son of a bitch, I thought. Why didn't you tell me, and I felt like calling him wherever he was and saying, Bernie for crissakes why didn't you tell me. You son of a bitch. And I felt like laughing and crying at the same time, over something all those years ago.

So maybe Theresa was five or six and Ted the year and a half younger, back then, when this thing happened that I still think about, and I remember it because they were home with Bernie, tucked in and safe and everything, and I had the job at Lakeside—closer to the side of the interstate than to the side of the lake—and it was Dave doing the cooking and me, and just two or three booths out of the eighteen being used.

It had to have been Sunday or Monday night, and it was raining, I remember. This steady and cold and miserable rain, and the trees were half bare already, and this was right before President Kennedy was shot, down to Texas, just two or three weeks before, I think. Because who can forget that. Exactly where they were when the phone rang or they interrupted the program on the radio or TV. Walter Cronkite wearing glasses, and you could almost see him wanting to cry. And who didn't back then.

So the two of them came in, the man and the boy, and we got plenty of people on vacations, or going from here to there, or from down to Boston or Hartford, the highway being so close as I said, so it wasn't out of the ordinary to see strangers.

But it was Sunday or Monday night, and raining steady, and it was well after nine because I remember thinking I had less than two hours in my shift, and I wasn't looking forward to driving in the rain and dark, and all those wet leaves lying there like ice, and my eyes doing tricks on me in the dark and the shine.

The boy was very pale like he'd been inside a long time, and his hair stuck out above one ear and in back. Stuck out the way Ted's did when he woke up mornings. He had on sneakers, I think, and this tee shirt, and jeans, and that's the first thing I thought. A tee shirt on a night like that.

And when I went over I saw the stain down the front where he must have thrown up, and the man probably rinsed it out in the sink at a gas station. It was just a stain the size of a man's hand, and brownish yellow, but you could smell it, and there's no mistaking that.

He had been sick, and his eyes were real bright like when they have a fever, and the two of them sat away from the big windows in front, and that made me think. Like who wouldn't want to sit near the windows, and watch the rain and the lights in the parking lot.

But they sat all the way back near the restrooms, and when I went over with water and silver and menus, he was real polite and spoke quietly. Said thank you and please, and I remember thinking he was a minister, and this was a boy from his church who had troubles and was being taken somewhere for help.

The man was thirty or forty, but maybe older or younger. His hair was short, and brown, and he had regular features. Brown eyes or maybe blue eyes. I was sure of brown for a while, and later I was just as sure of blue.

He had on one of those light summer jackets—golf jackets they used to call them, and a white shirt underneath.

He leaned over and whispered to the boy, and I couldn't tell what he said, but it was serious, and the boy's eyes almost filled up, and he was trembling like in a fever. And he was very very white like a ghost, with a little gray like a mushroom hidden from the sun.

This was a long time ago, as I said, and things were different then. I mean of course they were, that being all those years ago and such. But we didn't know as much about what happened behind closed doors back then. About the things some people did. We didn't know about the President and all the girls. The newspapers would never print things like that.

So maybe now I might do something different. Might make a phone call to the police or copy down the license plate number, or just ask a few innocent questions. Like where you from? Rough night out? Stopped over from the interstate, did you?

He would probably smile and say careful polite things, and I would have thought, No, it couldn't be. He's a youth worker from the state or a minister or something.

I guess I knew right away he wasn't the boy's father. I'm not even sure why. Maybe the color, or the shape of the nose or chin or lips. You just know somehow. Don't ask how.

Dave stayed in back, cleaning stuff out from the refrigerator, one of those big silver industrial refrigerators they were just coming out with back then. Dave was real proud of that refrigerator.

If he had come out and seen what I saw, maybe we would have called right away, and everything would have been different. But it was almost a week later when I saw the picture in the Boston papers, and that was only because some salesman or someone left the papers in a booth. And I happened to pick them up, and happened to turn a few pages, and there was the picture. He was smiling, and had on a sweater his mother must have made him wear for the school pictures, and he wasn't so thin.

But I'm sure it was him, and I felt almost sick to my stomach, and that's when I picked up the phone and called the state police, and then I called Bernie and said where's the kids, and Bernie thought I was crazy or drinking or something, and I said, Bernie! Where's the kids? This isn't for the fun of it, or such like that, and he said they were in their beds. They were tucked in and fine, and did I want him to wake them up to come to the phone.

I said, You're sure, and he said he looked in not five minutes ago, and my heart was going like crazy, but little by little it started to slow down.

And Bernie never said, What's wrong? Why you worried? Which was typical of him, and explains almost everything that happened between us later.

But that's another story, even though all of them are connected one way or the other, I guess.

But to get back, I gave them a few minutes, and brought a check to the Moreaus, to Mr. and Mrs. Moreau, who were still alive then, and came in once every week or two. They were sitting in front of the windows in front, and the rain was running down the outside, and I could see myself, my own reflection, and I saw the two of them in the booth in back. Not talking, and the kid hardly moving at all.

So I left the check for the Moreaus, and went back, and he said, We'll take the special, and that was fries and a burger, chips and a pickle, and Coke for the young fellow, I remember that. Young fellow, he called him, and

19

that wasn't something you heard.

I said, Two specials? And he didn't seem to understand what I was asking, and I said, You each want a special? And I could smell the shirt, and I saw dirt on his neck and the backs of his hands, and I thought something was really wrong, something here didn't fit.

He wouldn't look up at me, and I kept looking from one to the other of them, and the man said, Yes, that's correct, and I remember that exactly. Yes, that's correct, like a doctor or minister, and again I thought, he's taking the boy somewhere, maybe to protect him, or his mother or father died, or he wouldn't go to school.

The boy kept looking down at the table or at his hands, that were really dirty, and I said the washroom's right there if you want to clean up, and the man didn't look at me, and the boy kept staring down. And finally the man looked over, looked up—the man this was—and he said, That will be fine, and his eyes weren't minister's eyes or doctor's eyes. They were something else.

This was almost halfway between Waterville and Bangor, next to Newport and Sebasticook Lake, and there were even fewer people back then than there are now. We had miles and miles of trees and lakes and almost no roads, and this was three or four hours from Portsmouth, New Hampshire, and maybe six hours from Boston, but it felt like a thousand miles because there were beavers and moose, and nobody from here went down even to Waterville very much. And it was dark and it was raining, and this was middle or late October, and autumn comes early in Maine. Believe me.

So they could have gone just about anywhere, after the Friday he took him, and that's what they did. There were at least two days between that night in Maine, and when he disappeared in Boston, and they could have gone anywhere. Could have gone west and south—to Connecticut, then maybe New York, then east and north again. Across Vermont and New Hampshire. Maybe they stayed in the car, or they might have taken a room at a motor court.

I thought about all of that later, and have been thinking about it ever since. I mean not every day or week or even month, but more than you'd think.

They were there maybe twenty, thirty minutes at the most. Dave got the plates, the fries and burgers, and I brought them over, and I put extra chips out for the boy. And he sat there, small and whitish-gray, and I thought he was seven or eight, not nine or ten like I later found out. And they ate fast, and didn't say anything, and then they paid and left. And he left a tip. Ten or fifteen cents, which was more than it is today.

And he had those bright bright eyes almost like lights inside, and the man put his hand at the back of the boy's neck when they were walking out. Friendly, but maybe not friendly.

When the investigator came later, after I saw that picture and called, he said it might have been him. He said they could never be sure of course, and they had other calls and other reports, and it was days later. So the two of them could have gone to some cabin way up north toward Millinocket or Caribou even, and that's about as far as a human being can go without dropping off the side of the world. There're bears and otters, and millions of acres of trees and lakes and no roads at all. Even the old logging roads, a lot of them, were grown over and closed, and they'd need an airplane and helicopter and it'd still be like looking for a corner of a postage stamp on a football field.

And I think, Well how would I know, and what if I called, and his mother down there near Boston, and looking in his room at night, and the bed empty, and the school shoes under the bed with the laces untied, and I don't know if there were others—a sister or brother or what, and there was nothing about the father either, so God only knows what went on there.

But you wonder if she ever slept, and what she thought when she went to the grocery store, and saw a kid his age, with brown hair and freckles and some man.

And each year going by, and him getting taller and taller, and filling out. Noticing girls, and wanting to join the Army or play baseball or go to college. Maybe become a forest ranger. Who knows.

With Ted it was easy, even though they always said boys were much tougher to raise. He never gave me any problems, and married Marie, and they have four of their own now. Four, if you can imagine. Down in Houston, and both of them working and trying to keep after four kids.

Theresa wasn't like that. Theresa didn't want to stay here; she didn't like Maine, and first she had the apartment in Boston, and then Florida, and now she lives with this real estate man in Phoenix, and he's almost as old as me, and wears the shirts with the top buttons undone, and gray chest hairs showing, and the hair on his head's black as coal, so you have to wonder.

Theresa always had the clothes and car and the trips to islands, but she talks too loud and fast and smokes too much, and you're never sure what she does for a living. It's something with sales or travel or realty. She calls it, Realty. And she's past thirty.

So I think, Maybe she'll be okay.

I met Allen, and who could have thought that. And I remember Theresa asking me why it got dark at night, and if the woods got dark too, and I thought, Where did this girl come from and how did she think of that.

And sometimes I picture him, and what he looks like, if he didn't end up somewhere in the middle of nowhere, in a million acres of trees, in that tee shirt.

Maybe it wasn't him. Maybe that was his father, but I'd be ready to bet everything it wasn't.

I told Ted once, when him and Marie and the kids came up one August, and he said, Ma, you think too much. Ted with the worry lines at the sides of his eyes and mouth, and kids and Marie, and I thought, He'd be four or five years older than Ted, and Ted was in bed that night. The rain was falling all those years ago in October.

[3] Jim

People will sometimes ask me, and I will never know for certain how I should answer them. First they will want to know where I am from, and because I still live in Newton, where I was born and raised, I will say, Right here.

Then they will ask if I have family, aside from my wife Janice, of course, and I will tell them no. I have no kids.

Any brothers and sisters, they will then ask, and to be honest, to be perfectly honest, I never know quite what to say. Even all these years later, some thirty years almost, and I will blush and stammer like some poor soul with a speech problem.

I should say no. Nobody. No brothers, no sisters, and that would be the end of that. Then perhaps I could talk of the Red Sox or Celtics or of the traffic in and around Boston. Move on to safer ground, so to speak.

But the idea of that feels wrong to me. It feels like I have put one more nail into my brother's coffin, and I have no wish to do that. None whatsoever. So I say, Perhaps I do. Perhaps I have a brother somewhere in the world. Perhaps he is out there, alive and well, and leading a good life somewhere. And they stare, and they will perhaps be wondering if I am joking with them, or if I have possibly had too much to drink.

You see, I would very much like to tell them, I had a brother once, and his name was Ford. I did not know him very well, I am sorry to say. I was only five at the time and he was almost ten. That seemed like a great many years at the time, the nearly five years that separated the two of us.

There is one picture of Ford and me, taken by our mother the summer before, and it depicts the two of us standing in front of the bunk beds the two of us shared. I am wearing blue and red pajamas, and Ford is wearing blue jeans and a white tee shirt. Ford has his arm around my shoulder, draped like a sweater or something, and we are both smiling broadly. Perhaps we were even laughing.

The picture is just a little bit fuzzy and out of focus. Maybe the light was not of the best quality, or perhaps Ford and I were even moving slightly as our mother snapped the photo. But he looks like a nice, sturdy boy, and I am looking up at him, for he is more than a head taller than I, and it is evident that we were fond of each other.

But this, I am afraid to say, is the only photograph I own which shows the two of us together. My mother may have a few others, but I am not sure. Strange as it may sound, she and I do not speak of him. Perhaps we both feel, in some peculiar way, that if we never say a word on the subject, he might well knock on the door some fine morning, when Mom has come over to visit us or when I am visiting Mom. We will look up, and a nine-year-old boy will be standing in the doorway, and he will be smiling at us in a way that is both shy and expectant, and all of us will know at once. Everything will be exactly as it once was, only none of the pieces fit of course.

Still, Mother and I never speak of Ford, nor of what happened.

Even Janice, bless her heart, is careful on the subject. But once in a great while, I will look across the living room as she sits on the couch watching a television program, and I will say, Janice, I can no longer remember what his voice sounded like. Or I will say, I don't think I would know him if I saw him now.

Ford would be older now, of course. Thirty-eight years old, thirty-nine in late December. I myself will be thirty-four in September. Perhaps he is quite tall, and very thin, and sports a mustache. His hair was darker than mine, I think, and would still be darker to this day. Perhaps Ford put on a good deal of weight, and he has a belly which hangs over his belt, and you almost think the buttons on his shirt will pop.

Ford would have white teeth and a nice smile, the same as in the picture. He would call me Little Brother, or Jimmy, or Jim, or just plain James. Nobody calls me James, and maybe Ford would be the first.

I remember some things, but other things I do not recall as clearly. I know we shared a room, and I know my father left when I was a baby. I do not think I have any memory of him. Perhaps some image of a large face leaning over the bed, and a cheek rough like sandpaper when he leaned over to kiss me. But I am imagining that, as likely as not.

I am certain that Ford had a small transistor radio, not much larger than a cigarette pack, and I clearly recall that he liked to listen to baseball on the radio. The Red Sox, of course. I also recall that he had white sneakers, Jack Purcell basketball sneakers, and I can still picture the sneakers on the floor of the closet, and the laces undone.

Ford also had a shirt that was dark blue, and had a

pattern of red and white alarm clocks on it. I think it was his favorite shirt, for some reason, and I seem to remember that he wanted to wear the shirt almost every day. I believe Mom had to almost force him to take it off and give it to her so that she could wash it.

Dad left Mom, for no reason that I ever knew. He was a few years younger than her, and I remember hearing that he would go to the horse track in East Boston, and I think he was a drinker as well, so it was not an easy situation for Mother. She worked in a bank, and she got some money from him, for a time at least, and Grandmother Scott—that is Mom's mother—she helped out a little too.

So this was not an easy time for her to begin with. But I think she was beginning to feel more steady on her feet, and I think Ford was very good about helping around the house. I believe he washed the dishes, and straightened up and helped look after me when Mom had to go out for one reason or another.

Ford was tall for his age, and my guess would be that he seemed a bit older than a mere nine. Perhaps he seemed eleven or even twelve. Mom could trust him, and she often did, and I don't think he ever let her down.

And then he was gone, just like that. Ford was there, and then he was no longer there.

This was in October of 1963. President Kennedy was still alive, though he would be gone soon too. And it was a Friday, I believe, which was also the day the President would be shot. And Friday is the day also on which Jesus is said to have died on the cross.

I was home with Mom, because I was just in kindergarten and went to school for the morning only. And Nancy McMillan from downstairs would usually have been babysitting for me until three-thirty, when Mom would come home. But Mom had not gone to work. She had felt dizzy when she woke up that morning, and she called in sick. That alone was unusual. Mom was never sick, and even if she was not feeling well, she more than likely would have gone to work anyhow.

Mom was better by the afternoon, and she was making oatmeal cookies, and listening to the radio, I recall very clearly. The smell of the baking—the scent of oatmeal and nutmeg and cinnamon—and the music of Beethoven on the radio. His dunh dunh dunh dunh. Very dramatic, of course.

Ford came home from school, and stayed for no more than a few minutes. I wish I could say I remember those few minutes. I wish I could say I remember that Ford came in and looked at me in a significant way, and made some memorable utterance. Or that he hugged me, or kissed Mother, or even shook hands with us.

But he came in, changed into his sneakers and jeans, took his bicycle from the garage, and went outside once again. He was planning to ride around. Perhaps he was planning to visit either of his close friends, Chucky or Dana.

Then he did not return. At dinnertime Mother called the parents of Ford's friends, and she called Grandmother Scott, and finally she called the Newton Police. She spoke to the patrolman who came to the house, and then he left. Grandmother Scott came, and stayed that night, and stayed for the next few nights.

Mother sobbed often during that first night. I can recall the sound of that very clearly, and I recall also that it began to rain late that night, and I slipped in and out of sleep and a waking state. There was rain, and Mother sobbing, and Grandmother Scott speaking in a quiet voice to Mother.

On Saturday, the next day, a Mr. Egan from the state police came to the house. Mother gave him a picture of

Ford, and he asked her about Father. Where he was, and how long ago had he left, and did he make any attempt at all to see either herself or his sons.

Mr. Egan apparently asked if Ford was reckless or unhappy or the type of boy who would be likely to go off in search of his father. He asked if Ford was careful in traffic. He asked if Ford would accept a ride in a car from a stranger.

More men came to speak with Mother on Sunday, and on Monday Ford's bicycle was found behind a store in Newtonville Square, not a mile from where we lived. The police brought the bicycle to the house, and Mother said that yes, she was certain that this was Ford's bicycle. There could be no mistake.

Day after day went by. Mother continued to sob at night, always when she no doubt thought that I was safely asleep. Ford's photograph was in the newspapers, and the police came to the house again. More days went by. The police did not come to the house so often, and Mother grew more and more quiet. She became slow and dense. It was as though Mother had turned to lead inside. She tucked me in at night, and said prayers with me, but inside she had gone away. She was hiding behind a thick layer of something, inside, where nobody could see.

Everybody at school was very soft and quiet and gentle with me. They treated me as though something special had happened to me. First my father went away, and then Ford went away. And the teachers all smiled at me, and touched me on the arm and hand and head and shoulder. They wanted I think to make sure I was there. And the other kids were almost afraid of me, I think. They seemed to feel that I knew a secret, and had a power of some strange sort.

One girl named Rhonda—I still recall her name—asked me on the playground if my brother was dead or not, and I didn't say anything to that. Her eyes I remember were bright with curiosity and excitement.

The word *kidnapped* came up, but there was no note, and Mother had no money of course, had none to speak of. The bunk bed on the top stayed empty, as though his being missing was always just over my head, and Ford's clothes hung in the closet next to mine for more than two years. Even if Ford had walked back into the door, his clothes would no longer fit him. I used to think of that. How he was nine, and then he went away. And how he would have continued to grow, even though he was not with us in the house. Time would still occur to Ford, wherever he was.

Perhaps Ford is dead. That is the most likely explanation. But there was never a body found anywhere. There were neither fingerprints nor bloodstains nor pieces of clothing. His bicycle was behind a store in Newtonville Square. Behind Woolworth's, near where they kept trash and old boxes and such. But other than that, not a single strand of hair, not so much as a fingernail.

Ford disappeared into thin air. He vanished without a trace. It was like a magic show. They asked Ford to step into a box on stage. The magician in the hat and white gloves closed the door. He waved his wand, tapped two or three times. He opened the door, and Ford was gone.

And then he did not appear at the side of the stage or seated in the audience. Nodding. Smiling. He did not appear the next day nor the next week nor years and years later.

As I have said, I was only five years old at the time. I did not know what this meant or if this was an unusual occurrence. Mother sobbed and she became more and more quiet. The people in school treated me differently. Every one of them was nice to me. And I would be a liar if I did not admit that I liked that.

Even now, when I know more about this, I do not know what to say or do. I do not even know what to think. I do not know if I have a brother, and I do not know what to say to people.

I think also about what became of Ford. I try not to think of that. Nothing good happened to my brother. He did not mean for this to happen. Of that I am most certain.

Once I would have liked to think that Ford ran away to join the circus. He became a rider of horses and elephants. He became a clown, and hid behind a big red nose and blue hair and giant feet. He would paint tears on his face. Ford traveled from city to city and from country to country, and every place he went, he made children laugh.

Once I believed that Father took him away, but the police located Father in a rooming house in Revere, near a racetrack, and Ford was not with him. Father may have died sometime in the late seventies, of an alcohol-related illness, and Mother did not speak of it. The Welfare Department would have buried him, I believe.

So Ford went somewhere else, or was taken somewhere by someone or something. For a time, foolish as this may sound, I thought perhaps this had to do with the supernatural. With ESP or a UFO, or some out-of-the-body experience. A boy cannot simply vanish. Perhaps a spaceship came down and they took Ford away. They had heads that were large and floated like balloons or some such thing.

Most likely I know is the fact that someone took Ford to hurt him. To use him for sex and then discard him. Or take him and adopt him in a way. Tell him lies and threaten to kill him.

Now I am older, of course, and I know Ford was just a boy, that he was just a small child really, if you think

31

about it. And I do not recall him too clearly. I think he smiled in a certain way, or blinked his eyes when he talked, or sat in a chair in the living room, his legs curled underneath him. But then I think, no. That was not it, and then the worst feeling of all comes over me, that I am losing him a little more each day that passes by.

[4]   He Imagines

Everything was dark or bright, and shapes were huge, and his mother's face was like the sun and the moon, and there were small plastic birds over the crib—blue and yellow and red and green birds—and they twirled slowly around and around, and he would go to sleep dreaming of the birds, and the sky was far away and deep blue, and the birds could fly forever. They could fly over mountains and oceans, and in green valleys and caves, but they always came back in time for when he woke up. Then he'd reach and try to touch them, but they were always just a little too far away, and he watched as they went around and around.

His Mom sang, Fly me to the moon.

She sang, London and Paris, and she picked him up, and laid him on a table in the kitchen, and she looked down and smiled, and made faces. She frowned, she smiled, she said, La la la la.

She said, Sweetheart, and she was taking off the wet diaper, which was warm and smelled, and she was wiping him with a damp cloth, and she looked serious.

Then she filled the sink with warm soapy water, and she said, My slippery bonny boy, and the bubbles were silver and white, and the water made funny sounds, made sloshing sounds, made shushing and slapping and squishing sounds, and he laughed.

Mom said, What's so funny? She put her face close to his face. Her eyes were big, and her nose was a sideways mountain, and her mouth smelled like coffee.

What's so funny, pumpkin? she said, and she laughed and made faces.

He laughed, and clapped his hands, and she sang, You say potato, I say tomato.

The water was warm, and she used a cloth to wash his arms and hands, his feet, his back and bottom and belly.

She sang, London and Paris, and fly me to the stars on a warm April evening.

She said, What are you grinning at, sweet pea? What are you smiling at?

She said, Yes you are. Yes you are.

She lifted him out, and laid him on a towel. It was dry and rough, and she wrapped its sides around him and rubbed.

Her eyes were wide and blue, and her mouth was big as a cave.

She said, My little lambchop. My dumpling.

She put her mouth on his stomach, and blew against his skin and made an exploding sound.

What's that, sweetie? she said. What was that?

Her face was tense, was alarmed, and he began to cry, and she said, No, honey. No, no, no.

She picked him and the towel up, and pressed him to the front of her. To her neck and breasts, her arms, her hair, which smelled of soap and lemon.

There, she said. There. There.

He was gasping for breath, and crying louder and louder, and she said, Shhh. Shhh.

She said, Okay, now, pumpkin. Okay there.

Shhh. Shhh.

There, honey, she said. There now.

She moved her hand on his back. She said, There, now. There, sweetheart.

She moved her hand on his back. She took his arm, his small hand, and pressed it to her lips. She kissed his hand. She said, Shush.

There.

Then she laid him on the table, and she put a new diaper on him, she dressed him in a jumper with gray elephants all over it.

She said, What does a cow say?

She looked at him, her face only an inch or two away.

What does a cow say, sweetie?

He says, Moo, she said. Mooo.

She said, The cow's a great big thing with brown and white spots, and the cow gives us milk. And that way, you can grow up to be big and strong. You drink plenty of milk.

She picked him up, and brought him through the dining room, into the hall, then into the room where they slept. There was her great big bed, with blankets and sheets and pillows tossed around like there had been a storm, and she set him in his crib, and said, Now you have to wait for Mommy's bath.

She laid him down, and the birds were twirling, and she said, I'll be right back.

She went down the hall, and he saw the ceiling, which was flat and white, and then he heard the water, and he heard her sing, London and Paris, and the water, and the pipes, and the bed was like an ocean in a storm, and the bars of the crib had beads on them, and he turned the red bead and the blue bead.

The water made water sounds. The water sloshed and

squished, and he waited, and the birds were turning, and the green one was farthest away, and could fly for the longest time.

Fly me to the stars, Mom sang. Fly me far away, and let the world, oh, let the world know that I, oh that I, am gone away.

Her voice was high and bright, and her voice could fly away, and the radiator clanked, and was very warm, and he could wait like a good boy. He could wait a very long time while Mommy took a bath. He would be quiet, and he would watch the birds, and he would see the picture of the baby, and of the man and woman on the dresser, and he would not be afraid, and he would not cry.

She would come back.

She would not go away for very long.

He heard the water slosh.

She sang, The meadowlark, the nightingale, the call of the skies.

He would not cry, and he grabbed at the beads on the bars, and he tried to reach the red bird, and then the yellow bird.

He made sounds like water sounds. He gurgled, and then he blew bubbles that were silver and white like the soap. He blew more bubbles, and he made sounds like water.

She was taking her bath, and she would come back very very soon.

He closed his eyes, and moved his arms and legs in the air. He waved his arms and legs like he was in water.

Then he heard a great splash, and the floor boards creaked, and she said, Coming, sweetheart.

She said, How's my sweet pea? Has be been a good boy?

She came in wrapped in a white towel, and when she

bent to nuzzle his neck with her nose, her hair was wet, and tickled him.

She took the towel off, and rubbed it in her hair. She rubbed and rubbed, and she was long and white.

She opened the top dresser drawer, and she put on bottoms, then tops, then she went to the closet.

Today we'll go to London or Paris, she said. We'll visit the Eiffel Tower and Big Ben.

She turned and smiled.

How would that be? she said.

We'll have tea with the Queen.

How do you do? she said, her voice strange.

So nice to see you, my dear, she said.

Then she put his hat and coat on, his boots and mittens, and they were in the backyard, and the wind was blowing, and there were great heaps of puffy clouds racing across the sky. Mommy was hanging clothes on the line, and when she pressed each clothespin down it made a funny sound.

She said, Don't go too far, and he was on his hands and knees, and was crawling on the brown grass and the fallen leaves, toward the white fence. There were stones and pieces of sticks, and small mounds of earth that were frozen.

He tasted a stick, but it didn't taste like anything, and he was holding onto the boards at the bottom of the fence. They were like the bars of his crib, only wider, and on the other side, between the boards, he could see the yard next door. He could see a small tree and a garage, and he could see a dusty window in the side of the garage.

A garage was where they kept cars. A garage was a house for cars, was the place where cars slept during the night. And there was a giant old brown house, and an old lady lived there on the first floor, and her daughter lived on the second floor with her husband.

They wore hats, and waved sometimes when he was playing in the sandbox. They stood near the fence, and called, Hello, hello, to Mom, and he turned and looked up, and they waved to him too.

Hello there, they said. Beautiful day.

Wave, honey, Mommy said, and he just stared.

She came over, lifted his arm, and flapped his hand at them.

There it is, the man said, and laughed, and the woman said, Isn't that something.

Mommy put him in the stroller, and she said, Okay now, buddy, and began to push him along the sidewalks. Cars the size of hills roared past, and he wanted to cry. They went whoosh and roar, and there were many many houses, and bare trees, and the wheels on the stroller made a nervous clicking sound. They clicked so fast he couldn't follow them, and they turned down one street with fewer cars, and a giant dog was barking.

Woof. Woof woof woof woof.

The dog was black, and it stood behind a chain link fence and went, Woof woof.

A cat made a different sound. A cat made a meow.

They went a long way. They went for hours, it seemed. There were more streets, and then more cars. Then there were stores, and people walked by, and a woman stopped and said, Why hello, and she was tall as a building, and she bent down and patted his head, and rubbed his cheek with the back of her hand. She wore a leather glove that was cold and soft. She wore glasses, and her eyes were wet.

Well, well, she said. Aren't you the darling.

She put her hand on Mommy's arm, and said, He's getting so big already, and Mommy laughed.

The woman turned and waved, and he was too tired to lift his arm and flap his hand like that.

The wheels clicked, and they went in and out of stores. The stores smelled like fish and bread. One smelled like clothes, and another smelled like soap. The men and women behind the counter smiled, and they looked at him, and sometimes they bent over or squatted down, and they said, Aren't you the little man. The sport. The tiger.

How you doing, fella? one man with a black mustache said. The man stared and stared, and said, Isn't that right? Isn't that right?

And later, they were clicking past the trees and houses again, and a dog went, Woof woof, and he was partway asleep. He remembered the sounds, and he remembered the bare branches of the trees, and he remembered how cold his face and hands were. They went down curbstones and up curbstones, and there was a hedge, and brown houses and white houses. Cars went by, and there were cracks in the sidewalk, and he was off somewhere else.

There was a cow and a dog and a black cat, and he was crawling after them.

But before he knew it, he was in the high chair in the kitchen, and his coat and hat and mittens were off, and his mother smelled cold like the wind, and like leaves.

She was spooning baby food to him with the silver spoon.

Open, she said, and he was too tired.

The spoon was touching his lips.

Peach or apricot or pears.

One bite, she said, and it didn't taste so bad.

One more, she said.

Okay there. Good. Good boy, she said.

And he was lying down in the crib, and his diaper was still dry, and he would sleep for a while.

How long could he sleep? And was Mommy very tired too?

But the cars were rushing by, and the dog was very very big, and the dog was growling.

The shades were down and the door was closed, and Mommy was lying under a blanket on the bed.

He began to cry, and she said, Honey, and her voice was halfway asleep.

He cried louder and longer. He wasn't wet, and he didn't smell, but the trees seemed enormous, and the dog had white teeth, and he cried louder and louder.

Pumpkin, she said. Sweetheart.

Shhh. Shhh.

But he didn't stop crying, and she sighed, and the bed creaked, and she was leaning over the crib, and she said, I'm very very tired, honey. I need to rest.

But he kept crying. He cried loud, till he thought something inside would break.

She picked him up, and he kept crying. She patted his back, and stroked the top of his head. He gasped, and cried more, and coughed.

Okay, she said. Okay.

She whispered, I hear you. Yes, she said. I know.

She laid him on the bed, near the middle, and put a blanket over him. Then she laid down next to him.

You're very tired, aren't you? she said. I think you're very very tired.

She looked at him, her face very close, and he could see her eyes in the dim light. She stroked his hair, and tucked the edge of the covers under his chin.

She said, I feel like that too sometimes. I get real tired like you.

She ran her hand over his stomach, and down to his foot.

You must be very very tired, she said. After a big adventure like that.

We saw houses and trees, and we saw loads and loads

of cars. Didn't we? she said. Didn't we?

She kissed his forehead, and he could feel her breath on his face.

You saw the big world, she said. The bright big world. You saw a dog, she said. Didn't you? A black dog.

What's a dog say, pumpkin? What's a dog say?

Woof, she said softly. Woof, woof.

She put her face at his neck, and whispered, Woof.

Then she lay back, and he could feel her weight next to him. He could feel her heat, and he listened to her breathe. Her breathing was deep and slow. Each breath took forever. And then he could feel his own breath. It went slower and deeper. And then slower still.

[5] Wendy

For a long time I couldn't go to sleep in a dark room. I couldn't stay at home alone. If Mom sent me out to play in the yard I could only stay for five or ten minutes, and then I would have to rush back inside. I wouldn't walk to school by myself, even though I was in the third grade, and school was only three streets away.

But the worst time was at night, after my Mom or Dad came in to say goodnight, kiss me, and shut off the light. The first time they did that, I lay for about two hours in bed, and I kept picturing what the boy looked like, and where he had gone, and I pictured the people who took him.

And I didn't even know him. I didn't know his name, didn't know anything about him, except that he was in fifth grade, and we went to the same school.

In the dark I kept trying to imagine if he had black hair or brown hair or blond hair. If he was tall, short, fat, thin. If he was pale or tan, had brown or blue or green eyes. I thought I remembered seeing him earlier in the hall at school, and he was walking alone near the end of the hall. He was wearing a white shirt and white pants, and he seemed very sad and lonely to me. But I don't think I could have known him or remembered him. He was two grades in front of me.

Then much later, in the late seventies, when I was in college, there were all these pictures of missing kids on the sides of milk cartons, and in the yellow pages, and on fliers pasted on walls and lampposts in the city.

MISSING, it said at the top, and there was always a picture of a smiling kid. The kids were missing from Niagara Falls, New York or Spokane, Washington. From Santa Cruz in California or from Cleveland, Georgia. They gave the height and weight, the hair color and eye color, the date of birth, the date missing. And I would always check that date in the almanac, in the perpetual calendar. Six, twenty-one, seventy-five, or two, eleven, seventy-eight. I'd find the year, and then the month, and it would be a Monday or a Thursday or a Saturday. Then I would picture everything about that day and that place and that child.

Say it was Morristown, Tennessee, where we had stayed when I was little and we were driving to Nashville. I would picture the hills and the red earth, and I would imagine the train whistling through the middle of town, very late at night or early in the morning. And if it was a Saturday I would think of cars going to downtown, or kids playing kickball or football or whiffleball in the streets. Or on Monday, people would be going to work or school, and everyone's face would be intent and set, their minds on business.

In Santa Cruz, California, I pictured the day as always sunny, and I imagined the scent of oranges in the air. In Washington State I thought of the day as rainy, and in Texas it was dusty. Then I imagined the month, and how warm or cold it would be. July was hot almost everywhere, and in March there was plenty of wind. It was like one of these Hollywood screenings where they asked you to choose from different possible endings to the movie. Did they die and go to heaven, or did they move to a farm in Illinois.

Maybe the kid was walking down the street, on the way to a friend's house, or on the way to school, or to a store. Maybe she was in the backyard, playing in the grass with dolls or balls or toy cars. Or she was at the mall, the grocery store, the pharmacy. Her mother was looking at something on the shelves in a store. Was checking the price, reading the contents or directions on a label, and the girl walked down to the end of the aisle, turned right or left, and then was gone.

Maybe they had stopped at a busy rest stop, on the highway between New York City and Philadelphia, and the boy went into the men's room, and his mother and sister went to the women's room. There were fifteen or twenty cars, and there were people sitting at a picnic table under some trees. Cars pulled in, left, people got in and out of cars.

Then the mother and daughter were back, waiting in the car, and they waited and waited. Cars pulled in, stopped, cars pulled out. I kept seeing this man's face leaning out the window of a car. He had brown hair, and he smiled, and there was a thin white scar under his left eye.

During college, in my freshman and sophomore years, I actually cut some of the notices out. I tacked one up over my desk. Missing, it said. A four-year-old boy taken from St. Paul, Minnesota. He was blond, had green eyes. He had been taken December 3, 1977. That was a Saturday. St. Paul, I imagined, was cold and clear and dry that day. The wind off the Mississippi River was brisk. The sky was cloudless that Saturday, was clear and deep blue.

His name was Tim or Rick or Tom. Funny how I can remember everything else, but all I remember of his name is that it was short, was only one syllable.

I'm still in Newton, all these years later, and at the moment, these last few weeks, I'm at home, waiting. I'm due sometime in the next week or ten days, and I'm tired and anxious and calm and impatient all at the same time.

I work as an M.S.W., as a social worker. Most of what I do is counseling in a clinic for families and children. And I counsel myself these days.

You're feeling ambivalent, I'll say to myself. This is an enormous change. How will you deal with the baby? With the complete change in your life? What does this say about your and Bob's marriage? Does it mean you're finally settled? Finally reconciled to your lives? To each other?

At thirty-five you feel your time running out, and Bob and I both thought, If it's ever going to happen, it better be soon. So I went off the pill for six months, used a diaphragm, and once six months were over and the pill was entirely out of my system, we began to use no contraceptive. Bob said it was like walking the tightrope with no net.

It's funny how this changes everything, shifts the way you think and feel. It fills you, and I don't mean that in only a literal way.

When we first found out I was pregnant, back in June, we couldn't sleep very much for most of a week. We kept thinking, This is really happening.

Okay, we said to ourselves. We're pregnant.

Okay, fine, we'd say, and we'd take deep breaths. In, out, in, out. All the way down to the bottom of our lungs. And bit by bit, we felt more relaxed.

Then we bought books about pregnancy, and we read and read. We'd chart the progress, the growth of the fetus. At six weeks it's smaller than a fingernail, at ten weeks it has arms, legs, tiny fingers. It weighs so many grams, is so many centimeters long. Then you count in pounds and inches.

45

Now we are utterly, utterly sure. We can't believe we waited so long. We can't bear the thought of this not happening. If something went wrong. If after all these months, after all this hope and worry, we should somehow lose the baby.

Bob is calm. He says, Relax. We'll be fine. But I read the back chapters of the books, the chapters where they discuss all the things that can happen. Toxoplasmosis, Varicella, cystic fibrosis, Crohn's disease. There are sections on bereavement, suicide, depression. Everything, of course, can go wrong, and I think of every one of them. When I read about something new, something I've not yet heard of, I'm almost relieved because I can now begin to worry about that one too. I won't have missed it. It'll be something I've considered.

But there's more to it. Much more. There's a whole world, a whole life, and I can feel it inside me. It kicks, it shifts, it even sucks its thumb. It can blink its eyes and swallow and pee, and it does all of that—it has its entire universe—in the middle of my body.

I get very very tired, and sometimes it's a little difficult to breathe. The baby is taking up so much space inside, it's pressing against my diaphragm. So I move slowly, and since Friday, I am no longer working either.

The house is quiet and strange to me during the weekdays. I had never been here so much between Monday and Friday. I never heard the clock tick so loudly, or the cat walk across the carpet, or noticed how little movement there was in the neighborhood. If plumbers are working in the house across the street and two over, then I notice. I see the van out front, and I see one of the men— the one with the ponytail—come out to the van to get pipe or tools.

Bob calls once in the morning, at lunch, and in midafternoon. He asks how I'm feeling, and if there's any hint of pains, and if anyone has called or if there's mail.

There's not much to say, but it's still nice to hear his voice. He is very calm, and I can almost feel my pulse slow down when I am on the phone with him.

I lie on the couch and try to read. I read magazines, and I'm reading several books about babies, and sometimes I wonder how any of us arrived safely into the world, and managed to grow up and become adults.

My hands are folded over my belly, which is big as an ocean now. It's this great expanse, and I feel the kicks, the elbows, the small and large movements. Way back, when I was just getting a belly, the first movements were butterflies. They were just wings fluttering, and I almost didn't recognize them as anything but nerves. But since then, they've become stronger and stronger. They are very clearly life. There is a person in there, and he or she is almost ready to come out and claim us, to take over our lives, and make us love her, and worry about her.

We don't know if this is a boy or a girl. We had ultrasound and amnio at seventeen weeks, and we asked them not to tell us. But both of us think for some reason that this is a girl.

My sister has two boys, and Bob's sisters both have boys. So we're thinking there have to be more X chromosomes in the gene pool somewhere.

We think so many things right now. She'll have brown hair or red hair, and she'll have dark eyes. When she's two years old she'll walk and talk, and she'll love it when we read to her.

I picture her at five, at nine, at fourteen. I picture her with long hair, with bangs and braces, with jeans and sneakers. Then I imagine her on her wedding day, and I imagine that she has a baby of her own.

It's amazing, all that you think of.

My mother doesn't say much about being pregnant.

She says everyone was pregnant back then, and they didn't make too much of it. They pretty much knocked the woman out, delivered the baby, kept you in for three or four days, and sent you home with a copy of Dr. Spock.

There were no classes for the father and mother, nobody on television talking about the problems of parenting, and God knows there were no fathers in the delivery room, cutting the umbilical cord. They were out in the hall smoking cigarettes and looking worried. They didn't sleep or shave. Then after twenty or thirty hours of labor and lots of screams, the nurse would open the door, stick her head out and say, It's a girl!

Almost half the time now I'm thinking of what this was like for my mother and father. She was twenty-seven when she had me, and thirty when she had Ruth, and my Dad was a year older. Dad worked, Mom was home, and that was that. At least according to them.

I seem to remember playing in the grass in the back-yard of the house on Highland Ave. And I think I remember Ruth being in a playpen. There are a few other things, too, things I remember, but not very much. Almost nothing for the first six or seven years.

I remember driving in the back seat of the car with Ruth, and it being very hot and humid. And then around second or third grade, I can remember almost everything.

Most of all I remember not sleeping in the third grade, and how I couldn't be alone in the house or yard for even five minutes. When the lights were off, even when we were in the den watching television and everyone was there, I always pictured the dark corners of the room, and the darkness under the couch and chairs.

In bed I pictured how dark the backyard would be, and the bushes that were close to the house, and how people could hide there and wait.

And that is probably the worst thing right now, the

worst thought of all. Even worse than the idea that the baby will be retarded or will have some terrible disease. It's the idea of the child being stolen, of the child being picked up and whisked away, and of never seeing her again. That is more, I think, than I could possibly bear.

This is something I will not talk to Bob about. I don't want to worry him, and I also feel that as soon as you mention something, as soon as you even say it is unspeakable and unimaginable, then you have both spoken it and imagined it, and at that point the thing becomes possible. Maybe at that point it even becomes likely.

So I think about that boy in Newton, all those years ago. I think of his eyes and hair and skin, and how soft and clear they must have been. That is what I notice about children. How fresh and soft they are. The way their eyes and hair seem to shine. And then I imagine him in the supermarket or in the park, and something happened.

Maybe he just walked away. Maybe his Mom and Dad were abusing him, and he couldn't take it. Or maybe he fell into a river or lake or ravine, and his body was just never recovered. Or maybe he hitchhiked to some distant place like Colorado, and somehow found a new family. They had a trampoline in the backyard and they ordered in pizza on Friday nights. They were nice to him. They grew to love him.

Lying on the couch in all this silence, my mind whirls around like that. I can be tired as a baby, and desperate to sleep, but it spins around and around, and I cannot make it stop.

What can you know about anything.

I was one year old, and two, and three, and four five six, and I remember next to nothing about any of that. Did somebody come along and take me away during all the time I can't remember? Did something terrible happen, and I've buried it so deeply it will never come out?

Paul Cody

And is that what it means to be an adult? You wake up at thirty-five, and you're ready to have a baby of your own, and you realize—as sharp and sudden as a knife—that your own childhood has disappeared, has gone from you, and you didn't even know, and can't quite remember all that you've lost.

[6] Elwin

Nine years. Concrete and steel, and glass that doesn't break, and here in southern Illinois the summer's so wet and hot the walls sweat. Everything smells of piss and mildew, and doors go clang, and televisions and voices echo forever, echo into next month. Up and down the tiers you see bars, and hands and arms between the bars, watching and looking and waiting. We have time. We do time. All the time we do time. Thinking about that, that this is time we'll none of us ever get back, is a killing and evil thought.

Hell is other people, Sartre says, especially if they're assholes like me. Like all of us. So we look at a mirror, and we waste and rot and smolder like compost, and the summers are the worst. You can smell everything then. You can see the mirror sweat, can see beads of moisture on your face and on the surface of the mirror.

Summer's when we use knives, and drink rubbing alcohol, and in the showers in June and July and August you don't bend over and you don't turn your back and you watch very carefully every word you say.

Eyes get yellow and bloodshot and fingers and lips and feet move all the time, and they have lockdowns two and three times a week, and it's a relief almost.

I stay in here in Segregation and sleep fifteen hours a day, and I read and read, and I write letters, and I listen to the voices and the footsteps, and the screws go by, and keys go jingle jangle, and I have so much time it's bad to think about just how much and how long.

Seven thousand days. A hundred and forty months maybe. A thousand weeks. A half million hours. Tick and tick and tick.

Breakfast at six, lunch at eleven, dinner at four thirty. Spoons and enamel plates, and no knives and forks, and strip searches. Fingers in every orifice, and you almost don't notice anymore.

Here on Segregation it's worse than the General Population. It's stricter, and that's as tight as it gets anywhere. This is where you come when the rest of the federal system can't handle you, and Segregation is where you come when General doesn't work. If someone's going to stick you, or if you're getting fucked in the ass and don't like it. Or if they think you're going crazy and stupid enough to go after somebody with a shiv or with your nails and teeth.

Crazies don't care. They can do major damage very quick. Nelson from C-block took a screw down, and got a finger in the screw's eyes, and the screw lost his eye. Nelson got beaten in a serious way. They took turns with bars and steel knuckles, and left him for five or six hours, then came back and beat him more.

Nelson is head-injured now, and sweet as molasses, and doesn't cause anyone problems. The screw had full disability, plus a few hundred grand for the eye, and everyone's happy. Nelson was here forever anyway, so what difference does it make.

I've known some people in here, and I've heard some stories. Everyone has stories that would make a person cry. And that's what we do in the little time we have around each other, in the yard, or when they let us out, two at a time, to get air. That's how I got to know Ellis, and why I listened to all his talk. I still try to figure out from all the shit he told, what was real and what was talk.

He was next door for just under a year, and from what I heard later, he came from Danbury where he was doing four years for taking a minor across state lines, and for having snapshots of minors that he had taken himself. The word got out, and Ellis took some hits, and they thought he wouldn't last long, and they brought him here to Segregation. Not that they're nice people or concerned about the likes of Ellis. Just that it looks very bad for an administration when an inmate gets killed. It looks like the authorities are not in control.

He was a big guy, and he let me have cigarettes some-times, and I let him borrow some books. He read Marx and Nietzsche, and once he asked me if I had the Bible, and I said no. Then they started pairing off Ellis and me for meals.

Ellis was a Shorteyes, which is what we call people who like children, and they don't generally last very long on the inside. Half the people in here were abused as chil-dren themselves, so it's like they can do some good in the world by making life hard for a Shorteyes. It's a little payback for what was done to them.

Someone wrote that the child is father to the man. Keats or Wordsworth or somebody. So if you take that child, and you fuck him, and give him drugs, and force him to give blowjobs, you're taking his childhood away, and you're taking away the father of the man.

A Shorteyes does a terrible terrible thing because he takes the place of time. He comes in, and he fucks a little boy or girl, and he steals them. He takes their soul and their childhood. That's what happened to everyone in prison, to half of them anyway, and that's why molesters never last inside.

Ellis never said anything about this to me, and I never said anything about this to him. I never told him I killed a person, and never said a word about the lake in Missouri, and Martha Knight, who lost her life, and why I'm in here.

He used to talk about moving around from state to state. He did construction work and he painted houses, and he said there were long periods when he could live like a monk. He'd rent a room or a trailer, and he'd hook on at a construction site, or he'd just stop at a house that was being painted. He'd introduce himself and say he was a painter with years of experience, and he'd say, Why don't you try me out.

I could work like an animal, Ellis said. He said he didn't mind heights, and he could stand there in the sun, on a ladder on the side of a house, and he could paint the side of a two-story house in a day.

He liked the way his muscles ached at the end of the day, and he said he lived very clean. He ate green vegetables, and he stayed away from alcohol and sugar and drugs for a while, and he went to bed early.

Sometimes he went out for a walk, and sometimes he went to a movie. He said he loved to go through neighborhoods, and look around, and later I thought, I bet you did.

He said he liked to imagine the kinds of lives people led behind the screened windows, and he said he sometimes felt like knocking on the door, and having some man or woman answer, and he said he'd imagine them smiling when they saw him. They'd take him by the arm or hand, and lead him inside, and it would be very nice.

There was a fan in a window, and the air was cool. A

lamp was on in the living room, and the furniture was heavy and dark. There was a tasseled lamp, and a radio playing some soft music. Some big band music from the 1930s or 40s. He said there were two kids, a boy and a girl, and the table in the dining room was set for five.

Then he'd tell about the meal. Every single thing they had to eat—the peas and the roast beef and the mashed potatoes—and even what they had for dessert. Ellis talked real slow, and we couldn't see each other when we talked most of the time. He was standing at the front of his cell, on the side near me, and I was standing at the front of my cell, on the side near him. All you'd be able to see were the hands and wrists, through the bars.

This was Missouri, he would say.

This was Ohio in nineteen seventy-eight. Or this was Oklahoma, near Norman, in the early eighties. Reagan was President, he'd say, his voice low, and I'd watch his hands gesturing.

Late at night was the best time to talk. The screws didn't move around so much, and there wasn't much noise anywhere. There weren't the shouts and screams, and the televisions were off. There was just the gray paint on the bars and the steel floor, and on the cement wall. Gray paint, thick as syrup, like the paint on a battleship. And not much light either, and he liked to talk.

He loved to talk. Really. And he could talk soft like nobody I'd ever known inside. He read books all the time, like a few of us in here, and he could tell stories.

Listen, Ellis would say, his voice as quiet as a stone, but just as firm and strong.

Don't believe anything you hear about me, he said, because not much of it's true. It's just a small part and it's all shit, for the most part.

He was getting out in a year, then he was getting out in two hundred and nine days, and then it was less than a hundred days.

Wait, he said. Watch me go, and I'll remember you.

And he did. He sent me a Bible in the mail, and two or three years after the Bible, he sent me a postcard with a picture of Chicago on it. The lake and the skyline, and he wrote, Hog butcher of the world, city of broad shoulders, where Sinatra saw a man dancing with his own wife. Love, Ellis.

You tell me.

I lie on the bunk for hour after hour. There's the toilet and sink, and outside there's cinderblock and bars. I sleep a few hours, eat, read, sleep some more. I sleep in the day and at night. I sleep afternoons, evenings, nights, mornings. I read Jane Austen, George Eliot, I read Tolstoy.

Ellis was next door for one year, and he did the same things I did. He slept, he ate, he read.

He said, Tell me about drinking, Elwin. Tell what that was like.

Tell about your favorite bar.

It was in a town I call Deadtree, I told him, but that wasn't its real name. There was a dying tree—a giant dying tree—in the middle of the town green.

How many people, Elwin?

Maybe four or five thousand. Two main streets that ran parallel, and four or five streets that intersected. That was the town center, the business district. Then streets that ran off in other directions, with houses and the occasional gas station and restaurants and stores. Car parts, liquor, a 7-Eleven.

There was a meat packing plant, and some grain elevators, and Deadtree was the county seat.

What was the name of the bar? he asked.

Pete's. It was a single long room. Always dark, and the air conditioning was on all summer, dripping above the front door. Signs for Coors and Bud and Old Milwaukee.

You went in and there were three booths on the right, then the bar, and six booths in back. Three on each side. Plus a cigarette machine, a pay phone, the bathrooms.

Why'd you like it? he asked.

It was cool and I could sit all day, and the beer was so cold it hurt your teeth. There was a bartender named Carol, and she was divorced and had a son who was six or seven.

He said, How much did you drink? What was the high like?

I drank all day. I drank fifteen, twenty beers, and sometimes late, I drank gin and tonic. I liked how everything melted away when I drank. Not having a job, and the tattoo of the scorpion on my arm, and Martha who I lived with. I'd say what I felt like, and I never was scared.

What scared you? he asked.

His voice was so quiet I sometimes wondered if he'd really said anything.

You tell me, I told him, and he said drinking was like being on the road. Was like getting in a car without a map, and going and going.

He said in Maine there were thousands of miles of roads that went through pine forests, and you could drive for a week and hardly see another car.

He said when he was very very young there were birds hanging over the crib where he used to sleep. Plastic birds that floated over him, suspended on string. Red and blue and green birds.

He said drinking could take you anywhere. And I almost told him.

Martha was skinny and had blond hair, and sometimes she hissed at me. You useless piece of shit, she said. She said, Get a job, and we drank some more, and she had pills.

She said there was a lake and we went there late on a Friday night. She said to take two pills. One black beauty, one blue Valium.

She took her clothes off and went in the water, and I sipped and watched her.

Elwin, you dumb fuck, she said. Come on in.

She said she wanted to fuck every man in Deadtree because I didn't know how to fuck her right and proper. She said her father used to fuck her, and then her brothers fucked her too.

Don't do this, Martha, I said to her. I said, I don't know why you're telling me this.

She was white and long in the dark water. She had brown nipples, and a patch of hair between her legs.

She said, Come in and fuck me, Elwin. Fuck me like you fuck little boys and your sister and your mother.

This was no sleep for two, three days, and the ringing in my ears, and the headaches.

Martha splashed and splashed, and laughed like a witch in a movie.

Ellis said, Who was Martha? and I said someone I used to know. Then I was quiet.

He said he wouldn't ask again.

She said, You miserable piece of shit, Elwin.

Then she said my mother used to fuck all the farmers and the colored in town. She said my mother liked to lie down on a mattress in the back of a pickup truck, behind the bars in town. And wait. For quarters and dollar bills.

And she laughed. She laughed and splashed in the dark water.

Ellis said he knew some things and it didn't matter sometimes.

I could see his hands, and I could see my hands. He said, You were in Missouri, and I said I was. Then he patted my hand.

After that he was gone. A day or two later. And I might have told him. Her in the water. The pills. The things she said. Back then, and all these years now to go.

[7]   Medfield State Hospital

Ford stayed on the floor in back, and the man drove for hour after hour, and sometime during the night, somewhere by the side of the road, the man climbed to the back and put adhesive tape over Ford's mouth, then wrapped the tape two or three times around his head.

He said Ford had been screaming in his sleep, had screamed, No, help, had whimpered like a dog or something, and the man said he didn't want people to get the wrong idea. He said it was nightmares, and that was understandable, especially after what happened to his mother and father, to his brother and sister. The plane crash, the fire, the bodies charred beyond recognition. It was a terrible thing what could happen to a human body. Fingers and toes, nose, ears, cheeks, all melted away like they were made of wax. He'd seen that kind of thing in the war, over in France and Belgium and Italy, and he hoped he'd never have to see that kind of thing again.

The first day he said his name was John, but later he said his name was Henry. He had brown hair, and he told Ford the future was uncertain, but one thing he could say for sure was that Henry and Ford would be together for a good long time, and he wanted to make damn sure

Ford was safe and sound, and would never end up like charred steak on a slab in a morgue.

Ford wanted to say he had no father or sister, and he didn't know why he was on the floor of a car where the carpet smelled like urine and gasoline and beer and oil, and every time the man stopped and came to the back, he kissed Ford on the lips and the neck, and ran his hand lightly on Ford's side, from his knee to under his arm.

Henry said, I love you, and he said they'd be alone soon, and one time, the second or third day, he began to cry and tell Ford he was sorry, he was so so sorry. He didn't mean any of it.

Ford thought Henry made a mistake, had found the wrong person. Someone else had a family that died in a plane crash, and Henry would realize that and drive him home, and that was why he was sorry.

Then he said, You little fuck. You ungrateful, lying little fuck, and he pressed his fingers so hard into Ford's upper arm that Ford writhed and jerked and kicked the inside wall of the car, and Henry began to press rags over his mouth and nose.

They smelled like what his mother used to clean the bathroom, like pine trees and ammonia, and he was swirling away, and the man was above him, was grunting, saying, Oh, Oh, like he was hurt, and something was rubbing Ford's lips, and he was a long way off and far away, and Steve says, Ellis, and he is I, is me, and Steve says, Ellis, and it's dark as midnight again.

He rubs my upper arm with something cold, and the needle goes in, and it begins to go through me. Prolixin and Haldol and other things too. Clear as gin, and just as warm, and Steve says, Come out if you want.

It's two a.m., two-ten, and late July, I think, and the night is cool like fall.

Steve says, Shhh, and hands me cigarettes and a book

of matches, and says, Be careful.

He says, Walk if you want.

Watch TV, you want, but keep the sound down. Real low.

He says, One hour maybe, then you try to sleep again.

There's fire inside, and my feet are long like skis, and I'm slower than syrup. I won't pour. Over the floor, and under doors, and no sound.

The TV's gray, and people smile. Their lips move, and the chair is vinyl, has chrome armrests, and they're cold as fish, and more slippery.

Only red EXIT signs over both ends of the long hall, and Steve in the office, and me in here.

Swimming light, wavering, and the walls have tall shadows.

Outside the window there's lights on other buildings, and no moon, and stars like tiny holes in the dark roof of the sky.

I can stand a long time, and not say a word. The air comes in, and I have years to live. Thirty-eight now, and a wave comes over me. Heavy water, and I can barely stand.

Here at this hour, and how much more time till they come in and click the machine off, say, He's gone. Fold my hands on my stomach. Close my eyes with their thumbs.

Ten more years, twenty, maybe thirty. Nice old man, easy as ice cream, as cake.

Send the body to the medical school for anatomy class. Find string of tendon, nerves, organs gone bad.

Trees way off there, and faint spots of light. Someone in the woods still. Squatting in all that darkness. A man wearing women's underwear. I'm your pop, he would say. Don't you remember me?

Your pop, your friend, your last best fuck.

He has no teeth and he waits and his name is Henry or John. George, Tony, Ed.

I want to go for a long time.

I want to say only this.

Before I go.

Before I fade, grow more silent, turn to leaf or stone.

I am very sorry.

Deeply sorry.

Had it to do over again.

Chicago like a jewel at the edge of a lake. So many miles of neighborhoods, of cars and streets and silent houses. Schoolyards, and lovely children playing. Shouting and running. Their eyes clear, their hair clean and shining. Skin like petals of flowers.

How come, Mom? they ask. Why because?

Because the man in the moon drives a green bus.

Because the people in China have black hair, built a long wall, eat rice with chopsticks.

Because your father said so.

Because we can't afford it.

Because Mommy and Daddy were not getting along, just the way you and Tom don't always get along.

Because God made it that way, and he loves you very much.

At night in bed they sleep more intensely. Sleep more deeply, with greater heat, dream in sharper color.

Someone in water, in blue blue water. No clouds, and coconuts, and monkeys in the trees. A bird big enough to carry him on its wings.

Why not, Mom? How come?

Because your father can't find a job.

Because that's the way life is.

Because she was very old and very sick, and now she's in heaven and no longer feeling any pain.

What if you said a prayer, and promised to feed Zeke

every day, and never forgot to flush. Would he come back then? Would that make a difference, Mom?

Maybe, maybe not. Probably he'll never come back. He's dead somewhere. He's with God now.

God loves him very very much. God loves him as I love you. With all my heart, with all my soul.

Loves him enough to take him away. To kill him.

Southern Illinois in summer. All that heat, that moisture, and the bugs. The mosquitos and blackflies, the roaches the size of small mice. Snap on the bathroom light, and they race for cover. Across the sink and toilet. Under the curling edge of the linoleum.

Henry sleeps like a stove. Henry is all noise and smells and weight. The bed sags on his side, and it's like sliding downhill. Rolling toward him.

He grunts and snorts like a horse. The beer can's on the floor next to him, and sometimes he wets the bed. Full of all that beer that turns to piss, and smells like ammonia.

The house so small it's not a house. President Johnson and the war on poor people. Big sad eyes. Ears and jowls all sagging down. All the weight.

Henry says it costs just forty-five a month. Not even a house really. Water falls in the kitchen when it rains. Leave plastic buckets there. Go drip and drip and drip.

A shower stall with rust stains, and that buckling, booming sound when he bumps into it.

The roaches at his feet. Their long brown feelers, like car antennas.

You little fuck, Henry says. I do for you. I get money, I get food. I take you around.

I do for you and you sit there and look at me with those eyes. Big saucer eyes, you little shit you.

You stinking piece of feces, Henry says. You brown, stinking, warm piece of feces.

Says no matter what he does, where he goes, you'll never be happy.

Always staring.

Big eyes like a deer in headlights.

Shoot the little fuck through the eyes.

Henry twists his face up, points his finger at his forehead, then at his eyes.

Bang, he says, and stamps his foot.

Henry slurps beer. Henry's throat bobs up and down and up and down.

He takes the top off the cooler, and his hand rumbles around in the ice. Says he's only got seven left, and if he catches you touching his beer, you'll wish your dead mother never met your dead father.

God knows what you do, he says. He knows every little move, and if you think he likes it, if you think he doesn't remember because it's late at night and dark, you're very wrong, my friend.

Think again, pal.

You're very, very fucking wrong, Henry says.

He calls it his lollypop, and it sticks out, and is swollen and red, and he says his lollypop is very very happy when someone nice licks it.

His lollypop purrs and likes that very much. A tongue going all around the top, and down on the sides.

And then his jewels in their jewel case. They like to be licked too.

Then put it all the way in his mouth and down his throat even. And he won't cough or gag or puke.

His lollypop will explode like a volcano, and the lava is white, and he purrs like a kitty.

Then he says, Pretty pretty boy. He strokes Ford's head, and says, You're so sweet, and if only you were this nice to Henry all the time. Make Henry purr like a pussycat, and leave his lollypop all tired and quivering and happy.

Henry loves you very very much, he says, and wishes only what's good. And how can it be bad to feel so good?

He's big as a stove, and smells like tuna fish and salty sweat and beer. Then he breathes slower and deeper, and the roaches move in the kitchen, over the dripping sink, and on the street, cars still go by.

Missing tailpipes, they explode, and people shout.

Fuck, they say. Motherfucking cunt, they say.

Lick my pussy, they say, and laugh.

Suck my cock, they say, and bottles smash.

Forty-five dollars a month, and Henry has a Ford Falcon with only sixty thousand miles on it, and they can drive a long way, they want to.

Henry stops, and pats Ford's head, his side. Says, When you gonna learn to love old Henry. Love him like you should.

Henry says, This, that, whatever.

He says they'll go to Mexico, and live on the beach. Drink tequila, eat pineapples and coconuts, smoke primo dope.

Gold, Henry says.

Fuck some nice brown Mexican pussy, he says.

You like that, Henry says, and punches him on the arm.

Then you might talk to poor old Henry. Stop blaming him for everything that's wrong in the rotten fucking world.

Steve pads down the hall, his flashlight beam on the floor. He opens doors, looks in.

He says, How you doing, in a voice as low as a whisper. He says, Try to sleep.

Then he comes out and says, Ellis, and I say, Steve.

He says, You wanna play chess? You wanna talk?

I say, Talk.

Me or you? he asks.

You, I say. You tell me.

He says he wants to finish the hall. He'll be back.

And up and down he goes. Opening doors, looking, once in a while saying, Shhh, sleep.

Esses like a steam pipe in winter. Ssss. Snakes curling in grass. Long wavery blades of grass.

He says they were all happy, the six of them, the kids, his mother and father, and his grandfather, who was mostly senile. Who said, Mother, oh, Mother, late at night.

He was Vincent, and he came over from Ireland when he was twenty-two.

He lived to be ninety-four. He had white hair, and wore flannel shirts. He used Aqua Velva aftershave every morning. He smelled like the ocean.

Steve was the youngest, and they lived on the top two floors of a two-family in South Boston, two streets over from Andrew Station. On the Red Line.

The oldest was Maureen, then Bob, then Maeve, then the rest were boys. Ted, Jim, then him.

But don't try to keep track of all that, Steve says. It's too many. Even my mother had trouble keeping track.

Every Sunday they went to the nine o'clock Mass at St. Bridget's, and then they got donuts on the way home. A dozen donuts, so each of them got one and a third donuts, and that was all.

On Sunday they each got to have half a cup of coffee too, with half a cup of milk, and Grandpa had tea with a tablespoon of whiskey.

Bob was an altar boy and came back late, came in ten or twenty minutes after everybody else, and his donut and a third were sitting on a plate, waiting for him.

His mother cooked scrambled eggs, and sausage, and everyone got one sausage each. And if you were still hungry after, you had peanut butter and bread.

When everyone was done, and if their father wasn't

working that weekend, they went for a drive to the South Shore somewhere. To a beach in Scituate usually. Lots of rocks on the beach. Maeve collected seashells.

Steve puts out his cigarette, says, You tired now?

What about at night? I ask. Where'd you all sleep?

Maureen and Maeve in one room, Bob and Grandpa, then Ted, Jim and me. And Mom and Dad, of course.

Separate beds?

Steve nods. He says, After the lights went out, we had these talks all the time. Mostly Jim and Ted, but sometimes me. Talk about girls, or teachers in school, or things people said. So-and-so's father was a drunk, or Jackie Boyle's sister was retarded, and in a special home, or Mrs. Janowski had a baby with only one arm.

There's a bang down the hall. Steve gets up, and then it's somewhere else. It's Florida, on the Gulf Coast, down from Fort Myers, and in a trailer.

The moon's huge in the evening. It hangs in the sky like an electric ball that glows, and the sun burns over the water, and the roaches are huge, and move less quickly, and make a crackling sound when you nail them.

The cars in the trailer park pull out early, for jobs in supermarkets and liquor stores and construction sites, and the woman across the way is Yvonne, and she has a boy just eleven, and her mouth is thin as a blade.

In lawn chairs on the gravel, and TV all the time, and beers hiss open.

She says you go on and on, and I laugh, and murmur, and she says she never met a man yet who wasn't but interested in just two or three things, and the sun's past the water. The sun's in Texas and California. The sun's rising in Japan, where all the jobs are.

What's that? What's that they're interested in?

She says, You come inside I'll show you, and the boy's watching TV, and doesn't even look up.

She says, Sure, sugar, and closes the door, and her mouth is wet, and everything comes down and off quicker than a spill.

She says, What's this? This all excited for me? And holds on to it, and she's wet down there too.

Slippery as a road in rain, and she smiles and says, You know what I mean now? You catch my drift?

After, she goes under like a stone in water. She's far gone and a long way under, and I get my clothes on in the dark.

The boy's watching TV still. It glows on his face like moonlight, and makes shadows under his eyes.

He's not tired at all, even though it's eleven. He's alert and restless, and his Mom might as well be in some other county.

He says, You want a beer, and I do, and he gets me one, and gets himself a Pepsi.

At this hour.

His name is Frank, and he's wearing shorts and a tee shirt with Harley-Davidson on the front, and his legs are long, and skinny as string.

He stays up nights till one or two. Likes to watch Carson and Letterman. Likes stupid pet tricks and the monkey cam on Letterman. Dogs pulling vacuum cleaners from closets, and dogs that sing, and the monkey that climbs the rafters with a camera strapped on its back.

His father's in Arkansas, working in Little Rock, and Frank'll spend the summer there, and he'll get a dog and a mini-bike, and they'll go fishing, and maybe drive to Six Flags Over Texas some weekend. Five Flags, or Seven Flags.

It's like the fourth biggest amusement park in the world. Has two roller coasters, and it's open almost all night.

Michael Jackson's got the Elephant Man's body. He

bought it at an auction for fifty thousand dollars. And he's got more animals at his house than a zoo, Frank says.

Do I know that?

Know what else?

Wanna know what else? Frank says.

His sister, Michael Jackson's sister, posed naked in Playboy or Penthouse, and she had big ones that were round as melons. Kids in school saw them.

Frank watched the screen, and Steve says, Ellis, and I say, Okay.

And I walk slowly back to my room, and the bed creaks, and the sheets are almost cold. There's no light. There's shades of black, and patches that look invisible.

Frank was watching the TV, and he said sometimes Yvonne let him have a beer, and he liked the taste a lot. He liked Bud, and he liked Miller too.

She was his Mom, but it was okay to call her Yvonne. That way they weren't Mom and kid. They were friends.

Do you like Bud or Miller better? Frank asked.

He said, I know what you and Mom were doing in there. Mom doesn't keep any secrets.

You were having love, he said. That's okay. That's not shameful or anything.

Frank watched the television. A blond woman said it would be warm and sultry tomorrow, so make sure your air's in good working order.

Frank said the kids in school were jerks, almost all of them, but a couple were okay. He said one named Alan came over after school, and once they even looked through Yvonne's underwear drawer.

Shhh, he said. Don't say I said.

Alan was two grades ahead and his mother was once a dancer in a club. In a strip joint. He said she was still pretty nice-looking.

You ever been to Disneyland? he asked.

To Sea World?

To MGM Studios?

There was this thing where you watched guys dive from windows after they set the house on fire. Then they made it rain real hard, and they had a flood. After that they made an earthquake, and a lot of people screamed. That scared them silly, Yvonne said.

She said maybe they'd go around Christmas one year. Just the two of them.

Or maybe he'd go with his father. Either way, he said. It didn't matter.

Alan didn't even have a father. His father might have been some John from years ago. His mother didn't even know. His mother was gonna buy a beauty salon, and she'd make a lot of money. She could make almost a million dollars every year. Alan's mother was Stephanie, and she had real black hair.

Yvonne said at Disneyland, at Christmas, they could rent a big hotel suite, with two bedrooms, and you could order anything you wanted from room service on the phone. You could have French fries, and Cokes, root beer, and Sno Cones. You want peanut butter and jelly or T-bone steak, you can have it.

Frank said, Yvonne said a lot of people didn't go to Disneyland on Christmas, so there weren't many lines. And on Christmas eve they had fireworks, and they decorated the Magic Kingdom. He said they even had snow falling and reindeer.

Do you know how fast the Roadrunner can go? he asked.

He said about a hundred miles an hour.

The night outside in Florida was wet as laundry in the machine. It was close and wet.

The night here is dry, is light. A breeze moves over everything, even over the man in the woods, squatting.

Still watching.

You ever gone that fast? Frank asked. Up to ninety or a hundred?

Sometimes his dad did. Late at night. Sometimes coming home, on roads in Arkansas. He'd be out somewhere, seeing some lady and having a beer or two.

One time Frank was with him, and there were no other cars out. His dad shut off the headlights, and they were going seventy and eighty and ninety. Everything was just dark and streaking past, and the two of them, he and his dad, they started laughing. And it was like amazing. It was better than TV.

[8] Joyce

They move me still. They make me happy to be part of this life we have, here on this frail planet. And I think of that every single day I spend in the classroom. Even after all these years and rooms and faces. The Johns and Bobbys, the Beths and Sarahs and Debbies. These children, I think, are the very best thing we have, the only important thing we really have, and that moves me more than I can say.

And I have done this now for thirty years, and it's stronger than ever. This feeling. Like I have them only for nine months, and I must hurry to get everything in, or else it will be too late. They will move on to the next grade, they will forget me, will forget what they were like. They will begin to be careful about what they wear. They will grow tall and will have their ears pierced, their voices will deepen, and then they will become just like the rest of us. And I want to stop them and hold them. I want to say, This is the best thing in the world right now. Look at the sun and the moon and the trees and the birds. And remember what they look like because they will never quite look like this again.

But I don't, of course. I am not that silly, nor foolish.

Nor romantic, I may add.

I like what they become too. They are good adults. They are responsible and decent, and often very interesting human beings. They grow up and become doctors and store managers and Peace Corps volunteers. Coming from Newton, as they all do, they have good parents, most of them, and good schools, I don't hesitate to add, and much is asked of them.

But enough of that sort of thing. My husband, Lamar, who is an engineer and very much has his feet on the ground, tells me I was a preacher in my last life, and I do go on, I'm afraid. I think sometimes I am acting very old, though I am only fifty-three.

Only fifty-three. Funny how I consider that only. When I'm seventy-five, I'll probably say I'm only seventy-five, and so forth and so on. But I jog and I read, and even though my two girls are already through with college, and Jan will be married next year, I feel like I'm waiting for the next thing to happen. I'm looking forward to the next thing, because I'm not at all tired, and I feel that none of this has been too difficult or unpleasant or exhausting. And you always hear how tough life is. How it wears you down, and leaves you bent over and bitter and full of sorrow.

That's not been my experience. Even when my father died, I felt somehow that I was being let in on one of the central mysteries, on one of the deepest and most powerful secrets. This will sound strange, I know, but when Dad was in the hospital, dying, hooked up on all these machines, I felt like his death, his dying, was this final gift to me and Mom, and to my brother, Robert. Like this was the final thing he would teach us, and even though it was terribly sad and painful, and even though we cried and mourned, there was this deeply sweet—almost bittersweet, I guess you'd call it—quality to the grief, and that's what I remember most of all. It was Dad saying, Here is my death. This will be my last gift to you.

One afternoon, during Dad's last few days, Robert brought in Tracy, his oldest, who was only three at the time. And I remember how Tracy climbed on the bed, and kissed his grandpa, then lay on the bed next to him. And it was amazing. This beautiful three-year-old child, and this man who already had the sunken cheeks and the hollow eyes of a corpse. I thought, This is it. This is the beginning and this is the end. And that day, for the first time in my life, I knew that I would have children of my own, and I knew that I would always be a teacher.

Which brings me back to nineteen sixty-three, and my first job at Carr School, when I was only twenty-two, and three months out of college, and two absolutely shocking things happened, one right after the other. And the famous one, the murder of Jack Kennedy, seemed like an anticlimax, much as I hate to say that.

Three or four weeks before the assassination in Dallas, my sweetest kid of all, my first favorite student—in a long line of favorite students—disappeared, and that nearly broke my heart. His name was Ford, and I swear I was half in love with that child. He was the youngest in the class, I remember, and had one of the highest Stanford-Binet scores, and he didn't have a father. He sat in the row by the windows, and he had freckles and blue eyes, and he wore a dark blue shirt that had white half moons or clocks on it. I remember how he seemed to love that shirt because he wore it practically every week.

I don't know why some of them do what they do to you. I mean you try to like them all, even the selfish ones, the mean ones, the whiners and smirkers and brats. And you're able to do that, to find the good in every last one of them. But some of them walk right up and smile, and raise their hand, and without even knowing it, they're already inside your heart, and they make everything inside glow. Whether you want it or not.

It's like you try not to fall in love with them, you protect yourself, but they come inside anyway.

Ford did that, almost from the first day. It was the blue shirt, and how confident and shy he was at the same time. How he knew answers, but he didn't always raise his hand because he didn't want to show off and grab all the attention for himself.

And the thing that really knocked me out, that stole my heart forever, was on the playground that first week, and Ford was captain for kickball, and he picked a boy named Francis first. Francis was one of those hopelessly awkward and unpopular kids, and Ford must have seen him lingering at the back of the group, and when the two captains started to pick teams, Ford picked Francis first. And you could see what that did for a boy like Francis.

I thought, This boy is special. This is a rare one. And I went head over heels, and that feeling's never left me. Even all these years later.

That must sound strange, I know. Falling in love with a nine- or ten-year-old boy. But I don't mean it in any weird or romantic way. It's like when you have a baby. Everyone always talks about how painful it is. The delivery, and then all these three a.m. feedings, and how you never sleep, and everything else. The expense, the worry, the bother. It's a wonder the human race doesn't die out, to hear the misery of it. But what floored me, and what nobody ever talked about, was the way you saw the baby, and you took her home, and you fell completely, totally, supremely in love with this little creature. You were crazy in love, and that was something nobody had ever talked about.

I think about this stuff all the time, and I talk about it with Lamar. He's a prince. I'm crazy about the guy, and thank God he's patient. That's when he says about me being a preacher in my last life. Like there's all this life before we even arrive here. I want to ask myself, What was it like back then? What did you think and feel? Was it amazing?

I would like to know what the sunrise was like in the White Mountains in New Hampshire, say around the turn of this century. Or what it felt like to be riding in steerage on a ship from Europe. To be fifteen years old, and desperately poor, and to know nothing of this new world, and to sail into New York Harbor in eighteen eighty or ninety. What were the slums like? How did it smell? Was there the constant chatter of foreign tongues? A Tower of Babel?

Lamar would say, Joyce, and look at me. Honey, please. Slow down. And Lamar would be right.

Don't you ever wonder? I have asked him, and he says, Sure.

About what? Tell me.

And he says, I don't know. He shrugs. He says he can't remember, but he's sure he has. And that's just the thing. His idea of it is something wholly different. To lie there awake at night, and to have your mind go so fast that you imagine smoke is coming out of your ears. There's that much heat.

But Lamar just goes upstairs at eleven. He shuts the TV off, or closes his book or magazine, then flosses and brushes, and climbs into bed. The light goes off, and then he's gone. Two, three minutes, and his breathing gets regular and slow, and then Lamar must be dreaming about blueprints or mathematical equations or the price of our mutual funds.

I don't mean that the way it sounds. He is kind and good, and I am very grateful for that. But we are as different as stone and water, as wood and air, and I accept that.

Lamar would never think about Ford the way I do, even this much later. It wouldn't do anybody any good, Lamar would say, and he would be right. What's the point?

And the point is that Ford would be thirty-nine or forty now, and I think of that. I think of him with a few strands of gray hair, and I think of him as tall. Maybe six feet, maybe more.

He had blue eyes, as I believe I've said, and he would be a handsome man. He would have kind eyes, lively and intelligent eyes, and I imagine different jobs he might hold. Perhaps he would have taught astronomy in college. He would have explained to his students about the Big Bang and Black Holes. Yellow Dwarfs and Red Giants, and the theory of the expanding universe. At night he would have scheduled a number of classes at the university's observatory, at the telescope. And one by one, in the darkened room with the open panel in the roof, Ford would have had each of his students climb the ladder to the telescope and see Saturn with its rings.

Notice the clusters of stars, Ford would have said. Notice that yellowish star, above and to the right of Saturn.

The student would look, and there it was, and he or she would think, Jeez, and would listen as Ford explained about other moons or other times in the history of the universe, thousands and millions and billions of years ago. It would make them almost want to believe in God, and Ford's voice was low and hushed slightly, and was taking them, every one of them, to a place they had never imagined.

Or Ford was a pediatrician, and he called his patients Cousin, and spoke softly, so he wouldn't scare them, and as he examined them he always held their hand, or moved his thumb or finger lightly on their back or wrist. A thumb pressing slightly at the base of the skull in back, and the child would relax so thoroughly that many of them would actually lean their heads into his side, and he would say, So you're a little sore there, at the glands under the arms or at the side of the neck, and the child would nod, would murmur, Yes, and would see his or her mother sitting near the door to the examining room, anxiously watching. But even the mother, or father perhaps, would find herself relaxing as she watched her child relax, and as Ford talked and asked questions.

Where'd you get those brown eyes? Ford would want to know.

D'you buy them somewhere?

And the boy would smile and blush, and Ford would ask him to press against Ford's hands—with each arm, with his legs—and he'd say, Plenty strong. No problem with this guy.

He'd say, You like dinosaurs? Play soccer? Got a girl-friend?

He'd say, You could be a doctor when you grow up. You could go to the stars.

Ford would have done something like that. Or he would have had five kids, and would coach Little League, or take his own kids and the neighborhood kids on camping trips to Cape Cod, or to the Green Mountains in Vermont in the fall. He would have owned a hardware store, and been decent to his employees, and joined the Rotary Club.

The world would have been a better place. Very very slightly better, but he would have brought smiles and a little more hope, and a microscopic measure of understanding. And God knows we need that.

It was October, and I was twenty-two years old, and just out of college, and he had dark hair, and a cowlick, and I remember thinking how I would do great things with this class.

Then on a Monday, toward the end of the month, Ford wasn't in class, and that morning, it was the twenty-fourth or twenty-sixth, I think, that morning Walker LaRoche called me down to his office and asked me if I'd heard anything.

I said, What, and he said Ford was missing, since sometime Friday afternoon.

His bike had been found in Newtonville Square, and the police had been called in, of course, but he'd now been gone almost three days, and there wasn't a lot of reason, of cause, to be optimistic.

I remember feeling angry and very irritated with Walker LaRoche.

I said, What are you telling me, he's gone? What are you talking about?

I said, That's ridiculous. That's crazy. Kids don't just disappear into the sky, they don't just evaporate.

He said, Joyce, please, the same way Lamar would later say it.

I said, He can't just be gone. What are you talking about?

Walker put his hand out. He put his hand on my arm or on my shoulder. I remember that very clearly, and I remember his office because it had that smoky glass, the kind you'd see in bathroom windows. And Selma Kaplan, Walker's secretary, was just outside, and I could see her shape through the smoky glass. I think she had stopped, and she was listening, and I think she felt sorry for me. She did, and Walker LaRoche did.

Joyce, he said, his hand on my shoulder or arm.

I said, I'm sorry, Mr. LaRoche, but that's the silliest, the most ridiculous thing I've ever heard. Boys, children, don't just go away and leave no trace. They're not birds, I said. They don't fly.

And Walker LaRoche just looked at me, and now I know what he must have been thinking. That I was twenty-two years old. That I was just three months out of college.

[9] Louis

Odessa, Texas is stark as stark can be, and Odessa in February, in 1964, was even more so. The wind blows, and the sky stays gray for day after day, and you stand there by the road and watch, and piles of cloud roll and cluster and move across the sky, and you think sometimes, listening to the wind and seeing the sky like that, you think you've come here to the end of the world, and there's nothing will ever change, and no kindness in nature, and the best you can do is wait and keep your eyes on the ground in front of you, and when the real big winds come up, keep a kerchief over your face because the grit in your eyes and nose and mouth will make you wish you'd never been born.

And February of 1964 was the same way as it'd always been and always would be. Oil was off then, and President Johnson was new in the office, after the murder there in Dallas the November previous, and he was always appearing in the newspaper and on television, that big sad face of his, and that slow way of talking, which made folks think he didn't have a lot on the ball. But Mr. Johnson could have sold Cape Cod, Massachusetts to the Kennedy family, and they were not born yesterday either, if you follow my thought.

So when that car pulled up in February of that year, a Ford Falcon, I believe it was, and had Massachusetts tags, I noticed and paid attention, as anybody with half a brain would have.

The man was driving, and there was a boy in the front seat next to him, and I looked out, and the man was saying something to the boy, and after that they sat a few minutes, looking over the trailer park.

It wasn't much to look at back then, and still isn't to this day. Four trailers aside from my own, with steps up to the door of each, and a piece of fence in front, which mainly collected dust. Two of the four were rented—one to a Mexican man and his wife and baby, and one to an oilfield fellow named Lance or Shane. I don't recall exactly, only that it sounded like a movie cowboy's name.

He left a week or two later, without saying a word and without bothering to collect his deposit either, and the place was full of empty soup cans and True Detective magazines and magazines showing ladies in the altogether. And I did not mind taking a look at those ones myself.

After sitting and looking a while, and probably listening to that wind, and seeing nothing but the road and telephone poles and power lines, and then miles of nothing forever, the man got out, and knocked on the door of my trailer, which had the Manager sign. I opened the door and let him in, and he said did I have a vacancy, and I said how long did he have in mind, and he said he couldn't be sure.

He and the boy—his nephew, he said—were moving around from place to place, and weren't exactly sure where they would end up and how long they'd stay.

The boy, he said, had just lost his mama and daddy in a car wreck in Rhode Island, and he'd been called in to take the boy under his wing.

We go here and we go there, he said, and I guess I'm trying to help him forget.

I told him I was very sorry to hear that, and I hoped the boy would be fine.

They're tough, I said. Tougher at that age than they'll ever be. They can bend without breaking, I said.

The man said, Isn't that the truth.

I asked him did he want to sit down and have a beer. Did he want to bring the little fellow in.

There was Dr Pepper, and I never yet met a boy who wasn't happy to see Dr Pepper.

No thank you, he said. They were right tired, and hoped to settle in, and get some rest, and look out at their options.

They'd been moving so much, he said, they'd barely had time to stop to think.

Maybe here, he said, with all that space on the horizon, that space running all the way to forever, he said, they could finally stop and think and make some plans.

They needed to figure where to go and what to do. They needed to settle, and maybe somewhere, he said, he'd find the right girl, and the boy would have a mother to come home to again.

That is my fondest wish, he said.

I told him that sounded fine to me, and I hoped he would do just that. Think and make a plan, then settle, and find a good woman for the two of them.

They took the last trailer on the right, the one farthest from the road, and I didn't even ask for any deposit. Just fifteen dollars cash for the first week.

We shook hands, and I gave him the key, and I said my name was Louis Bales, and he said, Henry.

Good to meet you, Louis, he said.

The boy, I said. What do you call him?

He said he called him Ellis. He said it was different

from what the boy's mama and daddy called him, but he wanted him to be able to forget and put all that behind him.

I said that sure sounded like a fine idea to me, and I told him it was surely a kindness, what he was doing for Ellis.

He said, Thank you, Louis, and started out, and I stepped out with him.

The boy was in the front seat still, and didn't look over, even when I smiled and waved to him. He was one somber child, but he had good reason to be. His mama and daddy dead on the road in Rhode Island.

I figured there was ice or snow, and it must have taken place at night.

Henry started the car, the Falcon, and parked in front of the trailer down to the right, and I watched them get out and bring some paper grocery bags inside. Three or four bags, I recall. No more.

Then I went back inside myself, and tried to get some sleep.

I was working then, as I still do now, at the hospital as security. Today I am head of security, and have nine officers working under me. Back then it was just me most nights, and Bobby Hackworth weekends, and nobody during the days. We didn't have the drugs, and even though we had plenty of drinking and people acting up, it seems they wouldn't do the kinds of crazy things they will do today.

Today they come in on drugs of some kind, and they attack a doctor or a nurse in the emergency room. We will call the city police in, and have them taken to a state facility where they are equipped for that type of behavior. And believe me, seeing a man on drugs who is trying to tear apart the entire emergency room and every person in it is not a wholesome sight.

I have seen the city officers use mace and their night-sticks, and trust me, that is the only thing they could do in that situation.

So that day, back in February of 1964, I went to sleep, and got up in the evening to watch news on television, and left in my car at a quarter till eleven.

The Falcon was parked next to their trailer, and all the lights were out, and I thought they must be very very tired. They were a long way from Massachusetts.

The stars had come out and there was a moon, the first I'd seen of either in a while. And I remember thinking how far away the trailer park was from Odessa, and how far Odessa was from the rest of the world. There was just utility poles along the road, and the wind and nothing else for miles around, and it seemed to me that that boy sleeping in the trailer there must be the loneliest and saddest boy in the state of Texas.

And I thought all that night, walking the empty hall-ways of the hospital, of my own Papa dying in the oilfield, and Mama working, taking care of old folks in the nursing home, working nights most of the time, and coming in mornings, wearing her white uniforms, and the special nylon stockings to keep her legs from swelling up. Tired as a slave, and getting cereal for me, and saying, Sweetheart, calling me Honey, and Angel and Sugar. Seeing me off to the schoolbus, and leaving her was like dying every morning of my childhood.

We lived in a trailer too, out on the north side of Odessa, near the fields and such, and the nights were the worst time. She hated to leave me alone, and she was careful about me knowing the police number, and knowing not to open the door to anyone, and knowing to keep all the doors and windows locked.

She'd say, I'm not trying to scare you, Louis, but you need to know that there are people out there who do not have your interest at heart. She said to call the police if I saw strangers outside, and if I heard noises late in the night. Noises that were not a dog or cat, or something snuffling about in the garbage like that.

The evening was the best time. I would be home from school, and Mama would have slept, and would be wearing blue jeans and sneakers and one of Daddy's old work shirts tied at the middle. She was a very pretty lady still, in those years. This would be the early to mid fifties, and there was Elvis Presley on the radio and Bill Haley and the Comets, and Patsy Cline.

Mama made dinner for the two of us, in that narrow little kitchen, and she would have me set the table, and always the radio was playing.

This is a new one from Mister Elvis Presley, the announcer said, his voice slow and southern, not like the radio voices today.

And that beat would start up, and Mama would move from side to side, and sing a little, along with the radio.

She'd look at me and say, Isn't he something, honey?

I'd nod and look at Mama, almost dancing there, and she'd be some other person nearly. Mama wearing jeans and lipstick, and smelling like soap from the bath.

Later she'd make me do my homework at the table, and she sat in the big chair in the main room. She sewed and read magazines, and said, C'mon, Angel, if she had looked up and caught me staring at her.

Around ten she'd change into the uniform, and I'd be in bed by then, and she'd tell me to turn my head when she took off the shirt and jeans.

She wore white underwear and a bra, and I'd sneak a look as she was pulling a slip over her head, or zipping the uniform in back.

Then she'd be in the bathroom a few minutes, and when she came out she'd say soft as anything, I want you

85

sound asleep, Louis Bales, before I leave this house, and I'd try to squeeze my eyes shut tight.

And usually I would drift away just a little. Sounds would come from a long way off—a shutter banging, a dog, the wind—and then Mama was leaning over me and saying, Sleep tight, sweetheart.

Mama would kiss me, and I'd feel her breath on my ear or neck, and I'd hear her go out. And that seemed to happen so fast. The kiss, the goodnight.

Then the door, the keys, the car starting up and the tires crunching gravel. Then no sounds anywhere except the wind and the banging somewhere and a dog. Maybe a bird would whooo-whooo for a while.

Maybe an owl or a mourning dove. I don't know for certain. I was never one for knowing about birds.

I was seven years old when Papa died, and Mama was just twenty-six. So we were both very young together, when I think on it now.

And those nights were the longest things of my life. There was an alarm clock that ticked and ticked, and there were sounds that the refrigerator and the heat made. Humming sounds and rumbling sounds, and clicks and sighs.

But mostly I remember the sound of the wind, and the sounds of cars that passed on the road. The whine of tires and the engine. I'd hear it way off in the distance, faint as dawn, and it got closer and bigger and louder. Then it would roar past, big as noontime, and fade and fade until it was dusk again, was midnight and one a.m., and just as quiet.

Sometimes, once in a great while, the car would slow down, and pull in. There was just our trailer, and fifty feet down, a trailer that rented to different people over the years. And the car would go slowly past, would stop once in a while down at the other place.

One time, late, a car stopped outside, and the engine kept running, and I could just about feel the eyes of the man behind the wheel. Looking at the sky, and looking at the house, and seeing no car around.

And one time the engine stopped and the car door opened and closed, and there were footsteps. Around to the side by the kitchen and main room, then down this end.

The steps moved slow as anything, and I must have stopped breathing for a time.

This happened more than once, I think.

Happened when I was seven or eight, when I was eleven, when I was fifteen and in high school.

There was a knock on the door. A few taps.

Someone banged on the door, stopped, banged again.

One time the steps paused under the window of the bedroom. Someone tapped on the glass. They tried to push the window up.

Then the steps went away. They went to the car, got in, went away.

All that night, in February of 1964, around the time the man and the boy came, I thought of that. Because there was nothing else to do while I walked in the hallways and made sure that doors were locked. At one and at three and at five in the morning.

And shortly after that, maybe a week or so after they arrived, Henry and Ellis were gone. And I think of that boy even now.

[10]   He Imagines

The man was tall and his voice was deep like thunder, and he always called the boy, Pal.

He called him, Sport.

Speed.

Buddy.

Zip.

Bunky.

He said, C'mere, Butch, and the boy looked around, and the man laughed, and Mom said, That's right. That's okay, honey, and she nodded, and the man was standing in the doorway, and he kept looking at the boy.

I won't bite you, the man said. There's better things to eat, and he laughed low like he was hissing. He laughed like rain falling.

The boy walked over to him, and the man picked him up, and he smelled like cigarettes and medicine. He put his lips to the boy's forehead and kissed him. He smelled like the outdoors. Then he rubbed his cheek and chin on the boy's face.

Sandpaper, the man said.

The boy began to cry. First his eyes got large, then he stared. He squirmed, and the man held him tight.

When he began to cry, the man said, How old are you, Speed? How old are you anyway?

Warren, Mom said. Please, Warren.

How old is he? Warren said. Is he a boy or a baby? Which is it? A boy? A baby?

You've frightened him, she said, and Warren said, Melissa, you'll turn him into a fairy. You'll spoil him rotten.

Mom said, Go on, why don't you, and he laughed like rain falling.

In the morning he was there, and his face was dark and tired, and Mom was humming as she made breakfast.

He wore slippers with holes in the front. His big toe came through, and he told the boy that was for air conditioning.

That's so my feet don't get so hot, he said. It lets the air in to circulate and such.

The boy watched him, and the man said, C'mere.

He opened his arms, and spread his knees in the kitchen chair, and the boy stood in front of him. The man put his hand on the boy's shoulder, then on his hair. He ruffled the boy's hair. He looked him in the eye. His eyes were brown.

I didn't mean to scare you last night, he said. That's not what I meant to do.

He looked him in the eye, and the boy looked down. The man's hands were in his lap, and they were huge, and scarred. The nail on one thumb was cracked. There was a cut on the knuckle of his other hand.

I didn't mean that, he said. I should know better.

Mom hummed. Eggs and bacon sizzled on the stove. The door to the refrigerator opened and closed.

In school, Miss Naylor gave them crayons and white paper, and she said they could draw anything they wanted.

Bill made a house with a horse tied to the side of the house. Susan made a man holding balloons, and Patty made a picture of a lake and hills, and small islands of trees in the middle of the lake.

The boy drew a woman, and then a boy, and then way off in the distance, in the corner of the paper, small as an ant almost, he drew a man. The man had orange hair, and a blue jacket.

Miss Naylor said it was time for Quiet Time. She said that first they would have their milk and crackers, and then they would take their blankets and spread them on the floor of the classroom.

She went out to the hall to get cartons of milk, and then she came back and set the cartons of milk on a blue tray. Then she took out the basket with the packages of crackers.

Candace spilled milk on the table, and William called her clumsy.

William, Miss Naylor said. William, is that nice? Is that how your mother and father taught you to act?

She took a roll of paper towels, handed one towel to Candace and one to William.

You can help Candace clean up, William, Miss Naylor said. That will show how sorry you are to have called her clumsy. It will show that you really didn't mean to say that.

The crackers were very dry, and they made crumbs fall all over the table. The milk was cold, and the straw made the milk easy to drink. The straw made it so they didn't spill milk on their chins and down the front of their shirts.

When the milk was gone, they made sucking sounds in the inside corner of the milk cartons by sucking when the milk was almost all gone, and Miss Naylor said that was not a very attractive sound.

She said, Bill, did your mother teach you to make that sound at home?

Bill shook his head.

All right then, Miss Naylor said.

She said, You don't see Judy making those sounds.

She asked them to brush the crumbs off the table using one hand to brush, and the other hand to catch the crumbs.

Very good, she said.

They threw the empty cartons and straws and wrappers in the barrel. Then they took their blankets from their compartments, which Miss Naylor said were like their very own mailboxes.

They took their blankets out, and spread them on the floor. The boy was near Judith and Ralph, and he lay down on his stomach. The floor was very hard, and hurt if you leaned on your knees or elbows.

Miss Naylor shut off the lights, and she said, Shhh.

She said, That's right, her voice soft and low.

She read to them from a storybook about a Little Lame Prince who went away to a castle that was high up and far away. His mother and father had died, and his uncle became king, and the Little Lame Prince stayed in the castle.

There were no doors, but only windows, and a kindly old lady who looked after the prince.

The boy listened to her voice, which was low, and he heard the other kids shift on their blankets.

Miss Naylor said that the Prince was very lonely and very sad, but he did not know how lonely and how sad.

He had always been like that, she said, and so he didn't know anything different.

When she was a girl, she said, she had three sisters and two brothers, and she thought everyone had that many sisters and brothers. She didn't know that some boys and girls didn't have any sisters or any brothers, or sometimes, just one brother or sister, or maybe two.

So the Prince thought all little boys and girls lived alone in a far, high castle all by themselves. And he thought all little boys and girls had no mother and father, and had uncles who were kings.

Miss Naylor was very quiet for a minute. The boy couldn't hear anything. He heard the radiator, and he heard someone turn over.

Then it was later, and he must have fallen asleep, because suddenly the lights were bright, and everyone was rushing around, and Miss Naylor said he must be one very tired little boy.

Warren said that too, after dinner. He said, You look tired, Sport. You look like you could use a good night's sleep.

The boy yawned, and felt very tired. He felt the way he usually felt when it was a special night, when Gramma and Grandpa were visiting and he was allowed to stay up until he could barely keep his eyes open. He would watch them, but then his eyes would begin to close, and it seemed like their voices were coming from a long way off.

Warren was wearing a black and white checked shirt, and he had been to visit a man in the afternoon, a man who was trying to help him find the right path.

Problems were like puzzles, Mom said. She said they were what happened when things didn't go quite the way you had planned, and when other things happened instead.

Mom was frying hamburgers on the stove, and she was heating green beans, and potatoes were baking in the oven.

Mom said, Honey, it's very important for Warren to get on the right path and to work everything out.

She said, Warren's here as an experiment. He's here to

see if we can live together and be together the way we were meant to be. That way life would be easier and better.

Warren stood up from the table, went to the refrigerator and took out a can of beer. He snapped the can open.

Beer was like soda, only for grownups. It had alcohol, but it was not like whiskey or gin or vodka. It was a little like them, but different.

Warren said, You wanna try some, Speed? You think you'd like that?

The can was cold, and it smelled funny. The boy tasted it, and made a face. He didn't like the taste.

Warren smiled.

Someday you'll like it, he said. Someday you'll like girls too.

After dinner, Mom cleaned up in the kitchen, and the boy was in the room where he slept, changing his clothes. Warren came in and sat on the side of the bed, and watched him.

The boy felt funny, being all alone with Warren. He felt that Warren was watching him, and was about to say something was wrong.

When he was alone with Mom he felt he could say or do anything, and Mom would smile, and call him Sweetheart and Honey.

Warren said, You don't like me, do you?

The boy was quiet.

I can tell, Warren said. I make you nervous. I can see you tense up when I'm around.

He could hear water running in the kitchen, and he could hear the wind outside pressing against the windows.

Well, Warren said. Is it true?

The boy shrugged.

There's something you don't understand, he said, and

maybe you're too young to be told. That's how your mother feels.

Everything in good time, she says, and I guess maybe she's right.

The boy turned away from the man, took off his underwear, and got quickly into his pajamas.

But you don't have to treat me like I'm nothing, Warren said.

He sipped from the can. He sighed.

Some people can't help the way they are, he said, no matter how hard they try.

He said, I've been in some bad places, and I've seen some terrible things. Things nobody should have to see or know about.

I've seen men drink perfume, and I've heard them scream that there were bugs crawling all over them, Warren said. I've seen them, Warren said. I've seen them locked up in padded rooms because they tried to hurt themselves.

And that's a terrible, terrible thing.

He said he'd slept on the streets, and out in the weeds.

He'd slept in parked cars, and in cardboard boxes in the alleys behind buildings. Rats came around during the night, and he watched them sniff around, looking for food. If he went to sleep, he was afraid they would try to eat him.

That's scary, he said. Nobody should have to go through that or see that. And nobody should even have to know about that.

Especially a boy. Especially a kid your age, he said.

He looked at the boy. He was handsome, the boy thought. He had dark eyes, and high cheekbones. But he was scary.

Warren said, I'm closer to you than you could possibly imagine.

He said, I know you can't understand that. You don't know what I'm saying. You don't know what I'm getting at.

His eyes were wet, and outside the wind kept blowing. The water stopped running in the kitchen.

But just remember what I told you. I'm a lot closer than you think.

Then Mom came in, and Warren stood up, and he put his arms around her. He was a head taller than Mom.

She said, It's nice to see you guys together.

Warren said, Yes it is. We've had an interesting talk.

Mom sat on the side of the bed after Warren went out. She said, You okay, Sweetheart?

The boy put his arm on her, and leaned his head against her side. She was warm.

He's a very nice man, Mom said. You'll get used to him.

She said, Wash up and brush your teeth, then I'll come in to say goodnight.

Warren was standing in the hall, and as the boy went past, Warren patted his hair.

Thataboy, he said.

Then he was done with the bathroom, and lying in bed, and Mom came in. The light was out, and he could see the dark sky out the window.

Mom lay down next to him, and he could smell her hair. Her hair brushed his face.

She said, This is very very difficult for you.

She said, I know that, Sugar, and I promise things will get a lot better.

Warren's been in some very bad scrapes these last few years, she said. He's taken some hard knocks, and he's changed a lot. Sometimes I don't even recognize the man I knew years ago, the man I used to love.

But he's trying very hard, and we have to help him as best we can.

She breathed in and out and in and out. Her head shifted on the pillow.

When she was a girl, she said, she never thought things could be so hard. She had no idea. None whatsoever.

Then she was quiet, and he listened to her breath. She lay there a long time. She lay there until he couldn't tell if she was asleep or not. And then he was dreaming of long echoing corridors, and he was walking, and all the rooms were locked.

[11] Marshall

In here, in Medfield, they are nice to me mostly. I talk.
They leave me to myself. Before, it was different.

Don't say that, Grams said. Don't say that. Don't say
that. I don't want to hear a word out of that dirty little
mouth. That smirking, disgusting little mouth.

Don't you dare. Don't think for a second, you little
son of a you know what.

Marshall, you ungrateful boy.

A twenty-seven-year-old boy. All Grams does is try to
love you and teach you. And what does she get? What do
you give her in return?

Marshall is a nice boy. Marshall is a good boy.
Marshall never hurt a hair on anybody's head, never hurt
a fly, never killed a mosquito.

Marshall, you disgusting.

Marshall, Grams loves you very very much. Grams
wuvs her Marshall, honey.

You little fuck. You sneaky, lying little prick.

You piece of shit, Marshall.

You gelding.

Who took your balls, Marshall? Who cut them off?

Did Momma cut them off? Grams wouldn't do a thing

like that.

Don't say that. Don't look at me. We'll send you to the loony bin.

Please, Mr. Ellis. Tell the doctor. I didn't do it. I didn't do anything. Tell them, Mr. Ellis.

He's big like Grams. He wears glasses like her. Ellis is in here with Marshall. The doors are all locked. Ellis is a nice man.

Grams has eyes like plums. They watch, and she has thick arms.

Grams lifts her arm over her head. She's standing there high as a tree.

Not me, not me, not me.

I didn't do that. Honest, honest, honest.

No, Grams. I didn't tell Momma. Not a word. No. Please.

Touch me. Touch me.

Momma wants Salems and she wants white wine. The one in the gallon bottle, in the green bottle. Four ninety-nine. Rhine wine. From the Fatherland.

A slow burn, Marshall. An easy slow burn.

I like your tee shirt, Marshall, Momma says. Blue looks good on you. It does things for your eyes.

You have pretty eyes, honey. They're almost girl's eyes. So so pretty.

What does Grams do to you? Momma asks. What does she say when I'm out?

The house is dark like night, and the light at the edge of the shades is knives and razors. The radio plays Lawrence Welk and Tommy Dorsey.

Dance with me, Marshall, Grams says.

The house is cool and dark, and the halls echo. On the first floor and the second floor, and even all the way on the third floor, where the ceilings slant, and there are four rooms, and where Marshall sleeps.

I sleep on a bed with pine cones on the headboard. Grams had a brother who is long dead, and this was his bed.

No, Grams. Please. I won't. Please don't.

What does she do? Momma wants to know.

Outside is hot, and the cars and trucks go by, and the light falls down through the leaves on the tree. The shade has a hole and flaps, and in winter the snow whispers, and the heat, when Grams is cold and turns it on, hisses, and slides along the floor.

She is tall as a wall. She has plum eyes, and she is strong like a Doberman. A Doberman will tear your throat.

Don't say that.

Mr. Ellis is big like Grams. He is in here too. He wears a sweater with a hole in the elbow.

Marshall, he says. Relax, pal. For God's sake, he says. Boo.

He sits down near the window. He puffs on a smoke. He wears glasses.

Dr. Vaughn would like Mr. Ellis. Give him Haldol. Give him Stelazine and Mellaril.

He is a sweet man.

Come over here, honey, Momma says. She pats the side of the bed, next to where she is lying down.

Marshall, she says. Honey.

Grams is out in the hall, standing behind a shadow. Grams has ears. A big pitcher and big ears.

Marshall, Momma says.

Momma wears a nightgown, and her hair is tired from being asleep.

Come over here, sweetheart, Momma says.

Momma has breasts through the nightgown. They are round and they have brown nipples. There was milk there, and when she falls asleep, her nightgown rides up, and her legs are spread, and that is where I came from all those many years ago.

Marshall was a pretty baby.

Marshall was a beautiful baby boy. He was Momma's treasure. He was the apple of her eye.

Yes, he was.

Marshall, Momma says, and she lights a Salem, and the big glass ashtray is full, and there is red lipstick on some of the dead Salems.

There is a mirror, and a fireplace, and the bed has a top part, to catch the rain or the leaves. The paint chips fall, and Grams says they can fall until she's dead and gone, and then she won't be alive to care, and we'll forget all about our dear old Grams, and then it will be too late.

Don't look.

Don't look at me.

You little.

I'll teach you.

Grams turns on the stove on top, and the coils make little noises, and they start to turn red, and Grams says, Come over here.

Get over here, you little ingrate, you little son of that filthy whore.

Give me your hand, she says, and she strokes her fingers on the palm, and says, Jesus Christ in heaven died for filth like you.

She says, Watch.

She takes the hand, and the coils are red, and she holds the wrist in both her hands, and she says, Marshall, and her voice is steam in pipes.

She brings it closer and closer, and my eyes swim, and it's hotter and hotter.

No, I didn't.

No, I won't.

Please don't, please don't, please don't.

I promise. On my honor, for as long as I live and breathe.

Grams loves you very very much. Grams wuvs her little Marshall bird.

Her lips are crooked, and the air whistles through her dentures. She has a white sweater, and her dress is like wallpaper, with pictures of flowers and vines and bees.

Grams had a husband who would have loved his Marshall very very much. Only he had to die a terrible death, and poor poor Grams. She had to lose her Lester, who was the best man in the world.

He loved you very much, Marshall, Grams says, and tears fall down the front of her big glasses, and her nose is big and fleshy, and crooked like her mouth.

He's in a box in the ground. Grams paid four thousand dollars for that casket. Four thousand American dollars.

Don't you tell me.

Don't you dare try to say to me.

That rotten, that filthy.

Grams puts white lotion on the hand. Grams says it will be sore for a little while. She puts white strips of cloth around and around it. She kisses it. She says it is a shame how clumsy and thoughtless Marshall is.

You silly little child, Grams says.

Momma wants Salems. She wants a carton of Salems, and two bottles of the white wine. Take money from her pocketbook, Take a twenty and a ten. Take something for yourself.

Grams stands inside the shadow in the hall.

This is my house, Ruth, she says to Momma.

You ruined my son, Grams says. You drove him to the bottle, and now you've made this one crazy and I will not stand by and watch this. As God is my judge. As the

Lord is my witness.

Ellis does not move for hours and hours. He smokes and sits and there are clouds of smoke around his head. He looks at me, and my hands hold my hands, and my pants are falling without a belt and my sneakers flap like bird wings without laces, and he watches me, and I won't say.

The store is three blocks over and two down, and the man says, Got an ID, ID, ID?

I show the one with the picture.

Two bottles, one carton, one Slim Jim for Marshall.

What does she say? Momma says.

You can tell me. I won't tell anyone. You can whisper in my ear. You can say it soft as air.

I won't tell. She will never know.

No need to worry, to worry. To fret and worry.

Late late at night the rain falls like it will drown all the fires and blow shingles off the roof and the shade flaps and flaps and Grams is snoring like a bear sleeping in a mossy cave.

You say that.

How dare you.

You filthy.

Little feces.

Little piece of excrement.

I should flush you in a toilet.

No, don't. No, don't.

Promise.

I didn't.

Did not. Did not.

Won't ever.

The man is big and there is light in his eyes and his teeth are gigantic like Mount Rushmore in the Black Hills. In the mountains, and glasses.

He laughs big. He laughs like a bear and a mountain.

He lifts me. One arm, one leg, and swings me around and around. The trees, the bushes, the grass, the back porch rush past.

Put him down.

Don't.

Stop.

Please stop, please stop.

He is funny. Ha ha ha.

He swings Marshall around and around. High like an airplane.

Marshall can fly to the moon and sun. Around, and he lets go, and Momma screams, Grams screams.

He says it was an accident. He says sorry sorry sorry.

The siren and red and blue light. Red, blue, red, blue.

They wear blue, and they say, Don't.

Careful. Careful.

Up we go. Up we go.

Onto your mouth and nose. Just breathe deep and slow. Breathe slow and steady.

They go fast and the noise is loud and it is cold like ice high up inside his head.

They are all around him. The big silver light above, and four or five or six of them.

Glasses, and the needle near his arm, going in there, and they say, Shhh.

Okay.

Please.

I won't.

She says she cannot believe this. She says this is a terrible mistake.

Come here, Marshall, Grams says from her rocking chair. Her hassock.

Here. Stand here. In front, and her hands on his shoulders, and leaning in.

You hate me, I know. You wish I was dead. You would

like to take a knife and other things.

There, she says.

The knife is long, and has a black handle.

Go ahead, Grams says. I know you want to.

Her eyes are big and there are tears rolling down behind her glasses.

All I do is love you and feed you. I take you in, and you don't know how lucky you are.

What did she say?

Blip and ping and hiss. They say, Marshall.

The nurse, the doctor. They are nice.

Good as new.

You're a brave little fellow. You're a real soldier, Marshall.

Do you like ice cream? Do you watch Fred Flintstone on television?

He lies and steals and has impure thoughts. He would like to do that with his thing. Even now, hanging there between his legs, he would like to.

The disgusting piece of feces.

You say that now but what about when I'm not here? I know what you say to her. I know what she wants.

In your bed. She wants you there, between her legs, where you came from.

Grams in the hall, late late at night. The rain and the wind outside, and up the stairs to the third floor, slow and quiet. One by one by one.

You little.

I know.

She holds the pillow over my face, and she pinches hard. She pinches my nipple.

No, Grams. No, Grams.

I'll show you.

I told you, and you wouldn't listen.

She held the pillow, and the rain spills outside and flaps the shade.

She's immense. She's strong as God. She's big, and if she told him once she told him a thousand times.

Get over here. Get in here this instant.

I told you. I warned you, but did you listen? What do I have to do to get through to you?

You're being gamey with me and I do not like it one little bit.

The light is soft, and he sits, and Steve says, Marshall.

The keys cling and clang, and there's mesh like diamonds on the windows. They keep you a long time and Mr. Ellis has a smoke, a Lucky, a Chesterfield, a Pall Mall.

You tell those lies.

She takes the pliers and she says, Would you care to repeat what I know you're thinking.

Mom says it makes her warm and sleepy and happy all the way through.

Daddy said, See how big it gets when you touch it. See how happy.

Daddy said, Now, and snapped a picture, and said, Now.

Don't worry, Momma says. He can't bother you where he is now. He can't bother anybody for a long long time. He'll have gray hair.

Don't look at me.

Don't you even think.

She says she knows how Daddy loves Marshall, his best boy in the world.

Flush down the toilet like the piece of excrement you are, and don't you dare say that.

Filthy thing.

They should cut that thing off you. How would you like that? That would wipe the smirk off your face.

No, please. No, please.

Don't.

I promise. Honest, honest. Swear to God I won't. Swear. Please.

[12] Jade

I was in my twenties, and living in New York City for the first time, so this was all new to me. New York is a long way from the suburbs of Wilmington, Delaware, and I was just out of college, and I think I also wanted to say Fuck you to my parents in as many ways as I possibly could. They wanted a nice daughter who would marry an engineer from DuPont, and live a few blocks from them, and I was like, No way. Plus this was the end of the seventies, the beginning of the eighties. Coke was still okay, and nobody had heard of the gay cancer, which later became AIDS. The worst that could happen was you might get clap, and you could get shots for that, or you might get slapped around or robbed. Once in a while you'd read about someone like me in the papers. A college girl from Georgia or Oregon or near Chicago who moved to the big city for one reason or another, and somehow got raped or killed or something. Like innocence of the heartland meets urban ugly, meets the savagery of the streets, and innocence dies. It was never as simple as that, but of course nothing ever is. In no sense.

I had a place that first year near 28th Street and Third Avenue, and it was more or less what you'd expect. Plenty of roaches, and very small, and a few windows that looked out onto a brick wall. It was on the fifth floor, and the stairway was poorly lighted, and smelled like piss and vomit. You'd hear traffic on Third Avenue constantly, cars and trucks, sirens, cabbies leaning on horns. There were also constant smells, constant stink. Exhaust and garbage, the air blown out from air conditioners in restaurants, the wet smell of cardboard left out for the trash. Even the rain smelled particular in New York City. Or you'd walk uptown, on Lexington or Fifth, and you'd start to smell flowers or perfume, or those amazing restaurant or bakery smells.

That was why New York City was so incredible to me. I was twenty-two and a few months out of Wesleyan College, and everything in the world was there. Gypsies and people from Thailand, Puerto Ricans, black guys with silky voices, cowboys with pale pale skin who looked miserable without the sun. You could get amazing meals at Indian restaurants for a few dollars, or buy a TV off some guy in a truck. It felt for a while like I'd never need to sleep again.

That first year I worked for a temp agency, and they got me pretty good gigs. Two months at an insurance office in the Fifties, filling in for someone who was having a baby. A month at the offices of the telephone company, two weeks as a receptionist at a record company. It always felt like you were pretending to be someone else— the one off having a baby, the one taking the seminar in Seattle so that she'd be able to move up in the company, the one who went back to Phoenix to get her mother into a nursing home. And because I was never going to be there very long, everything was always easy.

But I lived for the nights. That was when I was alive. I'd go home and have a salad. I'd shower, change, maybe take a nap. Then at nine or ten I'd go out, and that was when the city made me high. All those lights and smells, the dark movements, like cats hunting in the jungle. And as I said, coke was okay and nobody had heard of AIDS, and I had money from Mom and Dad. I could buy a gram, could afford to take cabs. If I missed work or got fired, it wasn't the end of the world. Most of all, I liked the bars, and the men in the bars. I was a nice girl from Wilmington and Wesleyan, so I wanted to fuck a lot of different men. And for a year or more, I did.

There had been boys in college, and one in high school, but I was bored with that. Nice boys who would be going to grad school or med school, who wore good clothes, who had parents like mine. They'd hold my hand and rub my back, and late at night, back in the dorm, they'd touch my breasts and tell me I was beautiful. They all smelled like Ivory soap and summers in Maine. And afterwards, they all said they loved me. New York was different, of course.

The first time, I stopped in a bar real close to my apartment, and it was busy and loud. Most of the people were in their twenties and thirties. I sat down at the bar, ordered a gin and tonic, and before my drink arrived, this black guy in a leather jacket said, Hey, sugar. He smiled in a way that was almost shy, and I immediately thought, Hmmm.

He started to talk to me, and he paid for the drink. He told me he was in some kind of retail work, and I think he said his name was Basil. And before we were finished with even one round, he was whispering into my ear that I was a very hot lady, that I was making him hard just sitting there, and he would very much like to fuck me.

I could feel his breath on my ear, and then he licked my ear. Just for a second. His tongue darting out, and saying, You've a very very hot young lady, and when I looked at him, he still had that shy smile, and his eyes were deep and soulful, and he smelled like cologne and sweat and leather, and I swear, I felt myself begin to get wet down there, could feel the blood in my face, and it was a jolt of warmth, of heat. I thought of The Wizard of Oz, and I thought, You're not in Wilmington anymore.

We kissed, there in the bar, and then we got up to go, and we were only a block from my building. We stopped in the middle of the sidewalk, and kissed some more, and he had his hand on my ass, and I felt at the front of his pants, and he was hard. We kept kissing, all the way to the bottom of our souls, and I could hear traffic going by on Third Ave., and people walking by, and it was like someone had plugged me in.

Then we were at my place, and we were taking each other's clothes off, and I kept thinking, This is amazing. I can't believe I'm doing this.

He was down to his underwear, which were those tight nylon briefs, and his cock was bulging out, the way they always do, and I pulled the elastic away from his belly, and took hold of it, and he was very hard, and I kept thinking, This is different, this is different, this is different.

Then we were on the bed, and he was inside me, and going in and out, and he came within a minute or two. And it was nice, the way they tighten up, and you can feel the length of them quiver, and those spasms like their soul's having a seizure. But then it was over, and he rolled off me. We lay there in the dark, for five or ten minutes, and he got up and went into the bathroom. Then I heard a flush, and when he came back in, he started to get dressed.

Neither of us said much. He finished dressing, and then we kissed, and he left. I stayed in bed, and started to touch myself, and I kept thinking of him in the bar, lick-ing my ear, and saying he very much wanted to fuck me, and then I pictured him in his underwear, those tight nylon briefs, and the bulge of his cock straining to be released, and I came, thinking of when I'd pulled the elastic away and took it in my hand.

And that was the first time, and during the next year or so, I did this maybe once or twice a week. With black guys and white guys, with men in their forties and fifties, with cowboys and Indians, with Italian and Irish and Jewish guys. And with one I remember most of all, because we didn't even end up doing it, and because of what he did instead, and I get shudders just thinking of him.

This was quite a bit after the first time, the time with Basil. This was in February or March, maybe even in April. It was raining out, and kind of cool, and I remember how in the city, at night and when it was raining, wet surfaces seemed to catch and hold the light. Puddles, and the pavement, and even the hoods of cars lying there and shining like spilled paint.

I went out very late, I think because I'd slept almost till noon. I was between gigs, and this was early in the week, a Monday or Tuesday. The bars were always a little less crowded those nights. And for some reason, I went down to around 18th and First Avenue, which was not a pretty neighborhood. I was doing a little more coke than usual, five or six lines before I even went out. In fact, this was sort of around the time I bottomed out. By July I'd be in Edgehill, getting rehab.

The cab left me at the corner of 18th and First, and I walked a few minutes, along First, then over toward the river. All the storefronts had metal sheets like a rolltop desk over the windows, and a lot of them were boarded up. The bars were small and had signs for Bud and Miller in neon in the windows. One sign said, LADIES INVITED.

This was around eleven, eleven-thirty, and the streets

were mostly empty. And that was different, because on Third and 28th or 30th, even at one or two a.m., there were always people on the streets.

The place was called Madden's, and it was the usual bar with a few booths, only there was no music, no ferns, and maybe four or five customers. I sat next to him right away, three or four stools in from the front of the bar.

He was big, had brown hair, wore glasses, and had on one of those tan canvas jackets with the corduroy collar. He looked over and nodded, then looked back down into his drink.

When my gin and tonic came, I sipped, and he ordered another. He turned and asked me did I want one more.

Just starting, I said, and smiled.

Then he went back to his glass, and it was another twenty minutes, at least, before he asked me did I live nearby, work in the city? The usual.

I told him yes, twice, and he said that was nice. He'd only been in the city a week or so, and he didn't think he'd stay much longer. It was too big and was wicked scary, and half the people seemed to be wackos.

It seems like they opened the doors to the funny house, and told everybody to get out, go to New York City, we can't look after you anymore.

Then he smiled and looked at his drink some more.

He didn't look at me much or for very long. He seemed real shy, and I always went for that. I said he was right. The city seemed like that to me too at first. But you meet people, and you make friends, and blah blah blah.

We talked a long time. He was from all over. From Boston and Missouri and Texas and Los Angeles. He was in the Army a while, and he worked as a logger in Maine, and he painted houses in Nebraska.

What's Nebraska like? I asked, and he said it was like

pictures of the United States at the turn of the century. Corn fields and wheat fields, and white houses and churches. Everyone in Nebraska was nice.

I'm nice, I said, and he smiled and looked down. And I'd be very nice to you, I said. Then I touched his arm.

We had another, and then another, and we didn't say very much. I asked his name, and he said, It doesn't matter. I said, It's getting late, and he said, Yeah.

He was staying at the Y, and the guy in the next room talked in his sleep, and he hadn't slept decently in a week.

Finally I said, C'mon, and he said, What?

We're going to my place, I told him.

We walked to Second, and got a cab, and the whole time he didn't touch me. I put my hand on his arm or shoulder, and I kissed him on the neck, but he didn't do anything.

Then when we were inside at my place, I took his face in my hands and kissed him on the lips, and he started to respond.

He was tall, and had big shoulders and very clean hair. His hair smelled like lemons, I remember. And he was shy.

In the bedroom, I turned the lamp on the night table on, and unbuttoned his shirt, and undid the belt and zipper on his pants. He took off his shoes and socks, took his jacket and shirt off together, and then he was naked. His skin was pale, and very smooth, and I touched him, and he was limp.

I started to undress slowly, and he watched. The buttons, the zipper, the snap on my bra. I stepped out of my loafers, took my socks and jeans off, and he kept watching me. He looked at my breasts, and when I pushed down my panties and stepped out of them, he looked at me down there.

I stood in front of him, and ran my hands over his chest. I took his hand, and touched it to my breasts.

You have nice skin, I said. You're very shy.

He put his fingers in my hair, and kissed my forehead. He was still limp.

You don't like girls, I said, do you?

He shook his head. Sometimes I do, he said. Just not tonight.

We lay down on the bed, and I said, You're a curious guy.

Do you bring men home all the time? he asked.

I lit a cigarette, and nodded.

How come?

I shook my head, and blew smoke toward the ceiling.

You like going to bed with different men?

Very much, I said.

But you don't know why.

I shrugged.

He was on the side of the bed near the lamp. His hair was shiny, and his eyes were blue.

I'm sorry, he said. It's not you or anything. You're very attractive. It's not that.

I smoked some more, and then he got up and went into the bathroom. I heard him flush, and then he came out. He stood in front of the dresser. He took a tube of lipstick, looked in the small mirror on the wall, then pursed his lips.

You mind? he asked, and I shook my head. I lit another cigarette.

He put the lipstick on slowly and carefully. The top lip, then the bottom. He pressed his lips together. Then he took the eyeliner, and then Ultra Lash.

He turned to look at me. He reached down, picked my panties off the floor, and put them on. They were very tight, and I could see that he was getting hard.

He said, I've never done this. This is new to me.

That's fine, I said. Don't worry. Go on, I told him. And I was twenty-two, twenty-three that spring.

Show me, I said.

[13]   Medfield State Hospital

That year, Friday afternoon was clear as glass, and warm, and the air smelled like lakes in northern Canada, and geese flying in giant Vs, and football on Friday nights. Girls in high school wore plaid skirts and knee socks, and blouses with Peter Pan collars. Boys wore loafers and chinos, and checked shirts. After school, in Newton, they walked to Newtonville Square, and stopped at Brigham's or Austin's, and drank coffee and soda, and smoked cigarettes, lighting them with Zippo lighters or matches, drawing the smoke in, blowing it toward the ceiling, then looking around with casual eyes, as though they'd been doing this a long time. Smoking was easy, they seemed to say. Smoking was nothing.

Ford left school at two forty-five, and half ran, half walked home. Miss Levy, his teacher, had told him when he was helping to carry a stack of books to the supply room that he was a very bright and capable boy, and that she had high hopes for him. You can do anything, Ford, she said, and I'm confident you will.

Miss Levy was tall and thin, and she was very young. His mother told him Miss Levy was a gifted teacher, and he was fortunate to have her for his class.

Miss Levy wore perfume that smelled like autumn leaves, and outside the windows of the classroom that day, the trees were bright, and the sky deep blue, and he couldn't wait to get home and change and go out on his bike.

He put on jeans, a gray sweatshirt, and sneakers. He rolled the right cuff of his jeans up because of grease from the bicycle chain. Then he went out back to the garage.

Mom was home, was watching television. Something about a man who got amnesia in a car wreck, and the woman who loved him. You'll find a way, a nurse in the hospital told him.

His brother Jim was building a fort out of soup cans on the kitchen floor. He was lying on his side, his head resting on the linoleum, and was looking between two cans. Campbell's Tomato and Chicken Noodle. The fort had three stories already.

The garage was damp, and the two windows were covered with dust and dirt, and everything smelled like rain and motor oil and dead leaves. He unlocked his bike, put the chain around the bar under the seat, and went down the driveway. The traffic on California Street was heavy, so he stayed on the sidewalk at first. The trees were tall and full, almost met overhead, and formed a tunnel over him. The dead leaves swirled under his tires. They seemed to rise and fall as he went through them.

Ford went left on Nevada Street, past the giant gray house, and then Carr School was on his right. He rode quickly past the parking lot, where some of the teachers were getting into their cars, then past the school itself. He went right on Linwood, and kept passing groups of kids on their way home from school.

On Walnut Street there was a dip, and Day Junior High, where he would go some day, then a traffic light at Watertown Street. There were kids from Day, older kids with bags and armloads of books, heading toward Newtonville Square.

He waited at the traffic light with a line of cars, and when it turned green he went straight on Walnut, and then he was in the Square. The Massachusetts Turnpike went through there, and so did Washington Street and Lowell Avenue, and there were dozens of stores. The high school kids came from the other side of the Square, where their school was, and on Friday afternoon, on a warm and clear October day, cars and people seemed to pour across the bridge over the Turnpike.

Ford locked his bicycle behind Woolworth's, then cut down an alley between a clothes store and a bank.

Then he was standing on Walnut Street, between two parked cars, and a blue car pulled up. The driver leaned over, rolled down his window, and said, You.

Ford looked, and thought the man meant someone else.

Come here, he said. He motioned with his hand.

Ford took a few steps forward, and the man opened the door on the passenger side, and said, Get in.

It's important, he said. Something terrible happened.

The man had brown hair, and wore a tan golf jacket, and he was as old as a teacher.

Ford paused, his hand on the door handle, and the man said, C'mon. I don't have all day and night. This is serious. Get in. What's wrong with you?

Traffic went around the man's car on Walnut Street. People were walking past, were going in and out of stores, and if there was anything wrong they wouldn't be just going about their business.

Ford got in, closed the door, and the man looked in the rearview mirror. Then he pulled out into traffic, and they were on Walnut, going past the library, a church, then past the high school.

There's been an accident, the man said. Your Mom and Dad are dead.

The sun was shining and the leaves were red and orange like fire, and on the driver's side the man had his window down an inch or two. The air coming in both windows was warm, and smelled like fall.

I don't have a father, Ford said.

They're dead, the man said. I'm here to take care of you.

Mom's at home, Ford said.

The man slapped him hard across the face with the back of his hand.

You'll be dead too, you don't watch out, he said.

You little fuck. You simpering little shit.

Then they were at Commonwealth Avenue, and the man went right. The car picked up speed, and Ford began to cry, and he remembered he'd locked his bike. When the man realized his mistake, Ford could go back and get his bike, and start where he'd left off. Ford took deep breaths, like he was running. He breathed all the way to the bottom of his feet. He breathed and gasped, and breathed some more.

The man said he was sorry. He said this was difficult for him too. I know it's not easy.

He put his hand on Ford's leg and squeezed.

They got on the Turnpike in Auburndale, and went west. The man drove fast, and looked in the rearview mirror, and after an hour or two, he got off the highway.

Ford cried for a while, then breathed and gasped, and then he threw up a little on the front of his sweatshirt. He could feel it soak through to his tee shirt.

He felt faint, and he breathed as deeply and slowly as he could, and then he seemed to go to sleep. He was drifting along the edge of sleep, and the man kept driving, and then it was dark outside like night, and all the cars

117

had their headlights on. He went deeper and deeper into sleep, and his mother was there, and he was in his room at home, and his mother was there and she was pressing a cool damp facecloth to his forehead.

The needle barely pricks the skin, and on the upper arm, in the muscle at the top of my arm, I feel heat spread, and soon everything will be quiet again. The men will walk up and down, and that boy won't bother me. He had freckles, and wore canvas sneakers, and there was a stain on the front of his tee shirt. A stain the color of tea. He won't get out of the way, and it is time for him to leave. Time for him to go back to sleep and be quiet, and stop all the fuss.

They will put adhesive tape on his mouth. The man will have pre-cut lengths of rope in the trunk of the car.

Or he will start over again. Ford will be on his bicycle, will be riding his bicycle, all those years ago in Newton, Massachusetts, just outside of Boston, and his mother will be at work and not at home, and his brother Jim will be staying with an old woman who lives nearby and who babysits for him when Mom works.

The day will still be Friday, October 25, 1963, exactly four weeks to the day before President Kennedy will be shot in Dallas. The day will be clear and warm, and the leaves will be in flame, and Ford will ride along Walnut Street, in the direction of Newtonville Square. Once there, he will lock his bike to a chain link fence in the alley behind Woolworth's. And then he will walk around.

He'll go into Woolworth's, will walk up and down the aisles. He wants to buy a scouting knife or a baseball glove or a candy bar. He'll see women in red smocks who work for the store. One of them will ask him if she can help him. No thanks, he said.

Then Ford went out, will go out, to Walnut Street, and he walked to the right, toward the Turnpike. There was a church, just before the bridge, and a wall and lawn in front of the church. Ford sat on the wall, and watched the people and the cars go past.

A few minutes later, say five minutes, he noticed a man lying on his side on the grass, his head propped on his arm. The man wore a tan golf jacket, and dark blue work pants, and black shoes. He had short brown hair, and when Ford looked again, the man was smiling at him.

Ford looked away. He saw a woman walk by, carrying a poodle in her arms. Two girls in plaid skirts went by, and then a boy wearing a checked shirt, with a sweater tied around his waist.

When he looked behind him the man was still there, only he was sitting up, with his legs crossed.

How you doing? the man asked.

Ford nodded.

The man stood up, and walked slowly over to where Ford was sitting. He said, Mind if I sit down?

No, Ford said.

The man said, I think I know who you are, and I've been lying on the grass over there, trying to figure how to break this to you.

Ford watched the man. He had brown eyes, and when he looked at Ford his eyes were almost sad.

What's your name? he asked.

Ford.

I'm afraid you're the one, he said.

This was a long time ago, and now I am not even sure of this. He was nine years old, would turn ten in late December, and he had blue eyes, and straight brown hair and freckles.

And the man wore a tan golf jacket, and he had a blue car or a green car. A dark color. Maybe deep red, almost burgundy, but covered with dust. He took pills so that he could drive day after day after day.

The heat swims through me, and I am glad of that. Dr. Vaughn says that pink papers, when they are signed by a judge, are good for thirty days. He says I may well be here longer than that, could be here for months. Some people stay for years, but the staff do not encourage that, he says.

Outside is warm like July, and my tee shirt sticks to my chest and stomach. There are scars on my knuckles and wrists and forearms. My hands are square, and my fingers long and thin.

Prolixin is just for the time being, Dr. Vaughn says. It is only for the hospital setting. This is a very very strong medicine, he says. Sometimes you will feel as though you are covered with plastic sheets. You will feel as though you are inside a dream.

The long whine of cicadas stops for a moment, and I can see the gray sky through the mesh. The sun is white, and the grass between the buildings is brown. Past the field, there's woods and hills. This is twenty miles from Boston.

Florida was wet like this. Florida had palm trees, and the giant leaves whisked when the wind blew. Florida had swamps and mosquitos, and the tar on the road was soft from the sun. The bars and liquor stores in Florida had neon sunsets and coconut trees, and they were near the side of roads, near swamps, and sometimes people walked off the road and into the trees and bushes and swamps. There were spiders and snakes, alligators.

An alligator came up on a woman's lawn and ate her German shepherd. In water they would bring you under, and then rotate like a corkscrew. Around and around. They lived to be a hundred years old. One hundred fifty. Maybe two hundred.

The motels had Vacancy signs, and TVs in every room. The air conditioner dripped water onto the window, and there were cockroaches in the bathroom. The light went on, and the fan went on at the same time. There was no window, and the tiles were cold and wet, even on the hottest days.

Cars went by all day and night, even all the way out there. Went whining and roaring and whooshing past. The airhorns on trucks sounded like train whistles at three and four a.m.

There was snow in Montana in September. It began near Great Falls, at morning rush hour, and outside the city, driving toward the mountains, the snow picked up, began to fall almost sideways. Then there were just two dark tracks in the road, going in each direction, and an hour or two outside Great Falls, a motel that looked like a ski lodge.

They had a heated pool that was separated from the dining room by foggy glass, and I dived off the board and did cannonballs, and a woman in a black bathing suit did laps, and she finally stopped and watched me.

Whose beautiful boy are you? she asked and smiled, and I said, Henry's.

Nebraska was brown and empty in the west, and greener and more hilly in the east. The Oasis had separate cabins, and was surrounded by pine trees. He had handcuffs by then, and used Vaseline, and said if I'd keep my mouth shut, if I'd just cooperate for once, he'd make it worth my while. He'd give me five bucks for the next Indian trading post we passed, and he wouldn't turn me over to the prisoners, who would love to fuck a nice boy like me.

Maine was pine trees everywhere, and huge rocks on the coast, where the water crashed, and sprayed us, even twenty feet away. Maine was dark, and rained, and there was a white bungalow, and he put one cuff around the radiator and the other around my ankle, and he said he'd be a day or two, but if I made any noise I'd be in the state home by midnight, with one cock in my asshole and another one in my mouth, and a line waiting outside the room. He said they gave you baloney sandwiches and tomato soup, and grilled cheese sandwiches for dinner. The shower was crowded with twenty or thirty kids in one room, and all those boys were slippery and covered with soap suds. They were strong, some of them. They came off the streets, and had tattoos, and they lathered up with soap, and they got hard, and said, Get over here, and you had to bend over. They took turns, he said, and I had no idea at all how good I had it, how lucky I was.

He got his coat on, and found his keys, and then went into the kitchen. He brought a box of Saltines to me and a bottle of water. He brought a can for me to piss in, and said if I yelled or screamed or made noise, I'd get fucked in every hole I owned, and I wouldn't like that. They wouldn't use Vaseline either, and they wouldn't take me for trips. So just hold still.

He went into the bathroom, came out, ran some water in the kitchen. He changed his jacket, looked at himself in the mirror on the door in the bedroom.

You think I look like James Dean? he asked. You think?

He said, You don't even know who James Dean is, do you? Poor dumb fuck.

He brought an apple to me from the kitchen. He knelt down on the floor and kissed me.

Give me some tongue, he said. For Christ's sake, could you give me a little tongue?

His face was rough, even after he shaved.

He said, Kiss your Daddy. C'mon. One more.

Then he stood up.

Two days maximum, he said. I'll miss you.

He went out, and I heard keys in the door. Then it

opened, and he said, I love you. Don't you forget that.

Then the door closed again, and his footsteps went down the walk. The car started, and there were ticks in the wall. There was a dog, a mouse, a cat. Water dripped, and the cuff made a hollow sound on the radiator.

A car went by, and sometime later, another car. There was a couch, a table, two windows. There was a doorway to the bedroom, a doorway to the kitchen, and one to the front of the house.

He said we would go somewhere else, and I would like it there. He said I wouldn't have to go to school at all. I could have a bicycle, and maybe he'd buy me a twenty-two. Then we could go hunting.

Inside, it got dark. Then it rained and I slept a while. Rain was tapping the windows, and the cuff was tight on my ankle. A car went by, and the tires in the rain sounded like applause on television.

I ate a cracker, then I ate the apple. I fell asleep, and then I woke up and it was still dark.

I listened hard, and I could almost hear voices. Mom said to be careful all the time. She put a damp cloth on my forehead, and brought me ginger ale to drink.

Then it snowed, and was still dark. I was with a girl, and she said she had no more money. She was in Baltimore, and the ocean was down the street, and she said, You can stay as long as you want.

In St. Paul, Minnesota the Mississippi River was wide, and along the banks of the river, there were trees and paths and a playground. The boy said he was very very happy. He loved the swing and the slide, and the jungle gym most of all. Did I like Larry Bird of the Boston Celtics? Did I like Michael Jackson?

When I turn on my side my shoulder hurts, and everything is slow. I'm underwater, and I'll stay a long time. Dr. Vaughn will say, You could simply tell me and then be done with it. There's no place to go from here, no place lower or sadder or lonelier.

You must be very very lonely, he said.

That's the worst thing. The thing I don't believe I could withstand. That horrible loneliness and isolation, he said. I believe that that would kill me. I don't think my soul could survive that. He smiled and folded his hands into a steeple.

The church was in Ames, Iowa, and had stained glass windows of Jesus on the cross and John the Baptist, and Jesus with a lamb on his shoulder. Outside was bright, and there were cornfields at the edge of town.

A red candle flickered near the altar.

Now I lay me down to sleep.

Now I close my eyes, and feel the soft breeze lift the curtains. She reaches over and pats my side, says, Sweetheart. Says, Honey. Says, Sweet dreams.

He said he didn't mind, long as I paid him, and didn't try to hurt him. Sometimes they twisted his arms, or put a pillow over his face and pressed down, or wanted to use pins or pliers, and they wanted him to take a cool shower and lie very still and try not to breathe.

Where did you go after that? Dr. Vaughn asked.

This was in Waltham, near Newton, and the room had a torn shade, and a brown spot on the bedspread, and cigarette burns on the bureau. They said a hundred a week, and they'd cash the check from Welfare, and make sure to turn off the hotplate, and the bathroom was down the hall.

And there's no fucking maid service, so clean your own scum from the bathtub.

They had pills and they had pints of wine and gin and vodka. The television next door was loud, and the bed creaked.

I said, I won't hurt you, I promise.

I said, No leather, no rope, no tape.

She said, Why don't you talk to me. I'd like very much for you to talk to me.

Did you go to college or something? You talk like you went to college and read books.

Hey, Professor. You talk like some professor.

The water dripped in Florida, and the lake was surrounded by swamps, and in Illinois the doors clanged, and there was concrete and bells. In the general population. In segregation.

What was that like? he asked. Elwin asked, the doctor asked.

I'd like to hear your side, if you'd tell me.

Tate said, Why do you do this to me? Why do I love you like this?

Magic Man. Magic Man.

Just close your eyes and breathe deep, and then you'll wake up and it'll be all over with. Then you can have all the ice cream you want. We'll give you a little something, a little medicine.

The air was cold and thin, and I could spin around and around like a planet in space.

He said, I didn't ask for this, you know. I don't have to drag you around, and do for you.

He said, I could press my thumbs into the front of your throat, and you wouldn't even wake up. And I could leave you in a dumpster somewhere. Behind a gas station, or out in the woods, in a state forest. Your body white and pale in the moonlight. Your eyes staring, and clouds passing across the face of the moon.

The nurse said, Breathe real slow and real deep. Just go slow. In, and all the way down, and her hand on his hand, cool like that, and smooth and warm.

Out, and slow, and this will be over, she said. You'll wake up, and this will be over, she said.

[14] Dr. Dean Welles

I tried to sleep whenever and wherever I could. They kept a suite for us near the emergency room, two bedrooms, a kitchenette, a bathroom and shower, and we always kept the shades down no matter what the hour or time of day or night. So it had the feel of a place underwater, with dim, artificial light. John Malcolm, a colleague, had been in the Navy, and he said it was very much like serving on a submarine. The same light, and the same strange feeling of artificiality. All the air was canned, the temperature was always seventy-two, and you could never really tell if it was seven a.m. or midnight or high noon. I guess serving an internship, particularly in the mid nineteen sixties, was very much like a stint in the military.

So we slept when we could, and the nurses in emergency would buzz us when cases came in, and we'd trudge down the hall, forcing our eyes open and our brains into gear on the way, and I'd always hope it wasn't something truly awful, a person so broken up that I'd end up killing him, or perhaps even worse, crippling him for life.

I was twenty-six, and just out of Cornell Medical, and I'd gone to Cornell straight from Yale, and to Yale straight from Greenwich, Connecticut, so applying for the internship in Iowa City, Iowa, was quite a reach for me. And I had done that on purpose, to see something else, another part of the country that was a good deal different from New Haven and New York City, where not everyone had gone to an Ivy League school, and where the division between rich and poor was not so great a divide.

As I said, I was only twenty-six, which did not seem young to me at the time, and this was 1966, and Iowa City was a very long way from New York City. Irene and I had been married less than three years, and Maggie was what—maybe a year old, maybe a year and a half. Stephen wouldn't be born until that spring. So everything was in front of us and life was good, and we had the whole world.

After two days on, sleeping in the submarine, and treating patients, and looking at my wristwatch to tell the time and the day and date, Irene would pick me up—at eight a.m., say, on a Wednesday morning, and Maggie would ride in my lap on the way home. Then Irene made breakfast—huge breakfasts, with French toast and sausage and eggs and orange juice. Then we'd talk a while, till ten or eleven, and we'd play with Maggie. And finally, at noon or so, I'd go to sleep in the bedroom, the shades drawn, the rest of the world a thousand miles away, and I'd sleep for twelve or fourteen or sixteen hours. I'd wake up the following morning, and Irene and Maggie and I would have a full day together.

Now I'm far closer to retirement than to medical school, and I live once again in an apartment. It's really a condo, and I own it, but there are neighbors next door like in Iowa City. Here it's an old couple who play Mozart and Handel on the stereo. I see them from the front walk, and we smile and say hello, but for the most part it's just me in this beautiful place. Two floors, carpets, enough closet space for a family of five. There are three bedrooms up, and more than enough rooms downstairs, but it still feels different from the house.

You spend enough time in one place, you begin to think it's the world, and the house in Elmwood was like that. Six or seven bedrooms, depending how you counted, three floors, and a yard full of beech trees and dogwood and silver maples, and the nearest neighbor was at least a hundred yards away.

First Maggie and Stephen go to college, then Irene leaves, and I'm suddenly fifty-seven years old, living in a house the size of a small castle, and all I have is my work. And I'd sit there in the evenings, after work, and after eating a microwave dinner. The light in the yard, falling through the leaves on the trees, would be mostly gone, and I'd think, What is this?

Stephen's married, and has a new baby, and Maggie's on the West Coast, working more hours than me, and Irene has an apartment downtown and has finally gotten her master's in social work. She has a job and a man she has dinner with and who knows what else, and I'm sitting there, the empty microwave dish in front of me, and looking out into the yard, and I start to think of my father coming home from working in the city on the six thirty-two train, and coming in the front door exhausted, and we'd hardly say hello to him. He'd have his cocktail, and I remember how flushed his face would get, and then we'd sit down to dinner. And then he was an old man suddenly. Then the stroke, and he's in a nursing home, and his hands are shaking like Bell's Palsy or Parkinson's, and I put Maggie or Stephen in his lap, and his eyes have that hundred mile stare.

What was he like? What did he think and feel all those years?

I try to remember being a kid myself, and almost none of it comes back. The house on the shore in New Jersey every August, and Dad with his shorts and black socks, and we'd say, Dad. Martha and Elsie and me, because he'd take us out to a clam stand, wearing those shorts and socks and his legs were white like a plucked chicken, and we'd say, Dad. Really, Dad.

I try to think of what we said or what I looked like, or what there was between us. Of course he loved me and I loved him, and of course he was proud I'd gone to medical school, and I always knew that. But sometimes I'll pause and catch a glimpse of myself in the mirror, getting out of the shower, and I'll think of how my skin is pale, and sagging, and my hands have spots on them, and I'll wonder how I got here.

Or I'll see myself reflected in a glass door at the hospital or in a window. Me in my white coat and glasses, the tie, the dark pants, the loafers. I look every inch the physician, and I'll want to see the boy I once was, the kid with tousled hair, with a baseball glove or a fishing pole or a dirty tee shirt, and it's not there anymore. It's like he's so far gone, if he ever existed, that he's almost from another species.

So I would sit there in the house, the yard growing more and more dark, and I finally said to myself, I'll sell the house, and buy a condominium nearer to the hospital, and that's what I've done.

Perhaps that's why I look back on Iowa City the way I do now, as an almost perfect time in my life. Irene and I were still very much in love, and Maggie was beautiful and healthy, and Iowa had hills and cornfields, and white houses and churches on every corner, it seemed. There was no crime to speak of, and even the university didn't seem so big then.

The hospital seemed worlds apart from what I'd seen in my clinical rotations in New York. There, we had had gunshots and stabbings, little kids so undernourished they looked like an appeal for funds from some Third World country. In Iowa City we had contusions and heart attacks and automobile accidents. One morning a farmer came in missing three fingers to a threshing machine, and I saw a child of three who'd been scalded when he pulled a pot of boiling water off the stove. You work in emergency long enough, you begin to see the world as a perilous place. But you work in emergency in New York City or Chicago or Phoenix, and you see the world not only as dangerous, but as malign, as evil. The things people are capable of, the things a human being will do to another human, are pretty hard to imagine. And I guess that in Iowa City, I began to forget about all of that.

So when the boy came in early that morning, at one or two, and the nurses buzzed me, I was sleeping heavily and was in the last six hours of a forty-eight hour shift. That's my excuse, I'm afraid to say, but it's not good enough. I know that now, but this was 1966, was Iowa City. I was twenty six-years-old and a first-year resident. The world and the place and the person were all very different from who and what and where they are today.

So I was dead asleep, and pretty powerfully exhausted, and I think it was Monday or Tuesday morning, a time when we could usually expect things to be quiet. The buzzer went off, and I trudged out, and there was a boy, a kid, maybe eleven or twelve, lying on the table in the treatment room. His tee shirt was all blood and rips, and his arms were bloody, and his jeans soaked, and he was wearing sneakers that were untied, and they were pretty heavily spotted with blood too.

The nurse and I started to cut away the kid's clothes, the shirt and jeans and underwear, just to see what we had. The kid was very quiet, and very pale. He had straight brown hair, kind of long in front and falling over his eyes, and he was in some shock.

The boy had fairly deep cuts on his left wrist, deep

enough so that he barely missed the tendon, and the flaps of skin were very cleanly cut, and he had cuts on his chest and arms and on his shoulder. Those cuts weren't as deep as the wrist, but there was still a good deal of blood.

We got vital signs, which were good, as I recall, and I was immediately relieved. We're not in danger with him, I thought. This won't be so bad.

We cleaned him up, and I put maybe five or six sutures in the wrist, and butterfly bandages on the other cuts. Then I started to check him over, and this is where I should have known. There were bruises, a few days old I would have guessed, on his thighs and buttocks, and some evidence of rectal bleeding. Worst of all, there was chafing, in a circular fashion, on his wrists and ankles, consistent with having been bound.

Alarms should have gone off, and today, believe me, they would. But at the time, I simply didn't think.

In the hall, I asked the nurse how the boy had come in, and she said he had walked in under his own power. He told her he had fallen through a glass door and down some stairs, and his uncle, whom he lived with, had gone to Ames or Cedar Rapids, looking for work.

He said his name was John Andrews or Walter Smith, or something like that, and we should have known.

I went back in, and the boy was still lying very quietly, and he barely looked at me. We'd put a sheet over him, but even then, I could tell he was quite thin, and something made me think he was older than I had originally thought.

I said, How you feeling, and he said okay.

You want to tell me how this happened, I said, and he said he'd gotten up in the night to go to the bathroom, and he took a wrong turn in the dark and pushed through a door that was glass, and then fell. He said he put his jeans and sneakers on, and walked to the hospital.

This was a crazy story. I know that now. But as I was standing there, looking down at the boy, his wrist in white gauze and the sheet over him, I kept having these waves of exhaustion wash over me. I couldn't see very well for a few seconds, and I swayed a little on my feet, and all I could think about was going home and getting undressed, and crawling between the sheets of my own bed.

I think I asked him when his uncle was coming back, and he said, In another day or two. Something like that. Then I patted his hand and said be careful in the dark, and in the hall I told the nurse he could go home.

Maybe she looked at me like I was crazy, but maybe I am imagining her look. But the boy was given some clean clothes, probably some surgical scrubs, and he must have walked out into the Iowa night.

Two or three minutes later, I was back in the submarine sleeping. And I never mentioned the boy to anyone. There was no follow-up appointment to take the sutures out, and as far as I know, no record of what became of him. Probably the name, Anderson or Nelson or Jones, was false.

Looking back, the cuts seem to me consistent with self-inflicted wounds, and the bruises, the rectal bleeding, the chafing, are all red flags for abuse. Clearly, he was trying to tell us something, even though he wouldn't or couldn't say it. And I didn't listen, of course.

Where he went and what happened to him is a mystery to me. I hope that he was all right, but that's probably a false hope. The truth is, I just have no way of knowing.

That spring, maybe five or six months later, Stephen was born, and we were somehow complete. We moved to a bigger apartment, and in my second year, the shifts became shorter. Twenty-four hours on, forty-eight off. At the time, that seemed perfectly reasonable.

We stayed in Iowa City four years. Then we moved to San Diego, spent nearly seven years there, and finally came back to the East in the late seventies.

Now I live in this condominium, and I work four days a week. I have more money and more room than I need. In the evenings I'll sit at the dining room table, long after I've finished my dinner. The light will be fading outside the window, but I won't turn any lights on inside. I'll sit, and look at the bushes and trees outside, and at the darkening sky. And I'll wonder if my father did this as well. In his lifetime. Before the stroke, but after all of us had gone.

[15]   Henry

The boy's a fucking liar. I'll tell you that right away. He lied about who I was. He lied about where we went. He lied about what I did and what I said. He even lied about the color of my jacket. My jacket was yellow, and I was thirty-eight years old, and I didn't force the little shit to do anything.

He even lied about how old he was. He said he was fifteen years old, and how was I supposed to know. He was maybe small for his age, you ask me. He had no hair down there at first, but sometimes they develop late. I have seen pictures of them sixteen, seventeen, and still no hair. So don't tell me. Don't even think to tell me.

The little fruit.

Fucking liar.

I get a pint of MD, and it will last me two, three days. All fuzzy and warm. A bunny. Outside the window are the park and school. Swing set, slide, bars where they swing and hang and climb. Little monkeys. Yelling and laughing. Sneakers untied, and faces red from all the running about. They need to let off steam, being cooped up all day long like that.

The teacher's a nice-looking lady with black hair tied

back all the time. She wears a blue coat, and she says things to the kids.

Watch out there.

Be careful.

Katie.

Honey, she says to one of them.

What with my hip, I do not go around like in the old days. I stand up more than a few minutes and the ache will begin. And soon, the hip will feel like hot lead in there, and don't you think for a minute that that does not hurt. The doc gave me pills, but MD works a whole lot better. That is my medicine, I tell the doc.

You watch out, he says to me. I will have to put you up to the VA for alcoholism, you don't watch out.

He is thirty years old at the most. College and after that medical school. Harvard I bet. He is a nice boy.

You lay off that stuff, he tells me. But what does he know.

You think Utah Beach was fun. The shells flying overhead, and the bullets. Nobody can know the feel of that, who hasn't been there. The noise like thunder, and dirt and smoke in the air. The smell of diesel oil and the stink of bodies and mud and everything.

Don't cry to me about your problems. Don't be a baby because you are crying on the wrong shoulder.

I told you, so just listen.

Welfare comes around. Lady with red hair and briefcase. This form, that form, a form for the state, one for Washington, DC, one for J. Edgar Hoover and President Bush and Jesus Christ too.

Then Carole from Home Health comes along. Does shopping and cleaning. Cooks food for the freezer, so later I will put it in the microwave.

I like Cheerios and I like Camel cigarettes with the pyramid on the package.

Dorchester was a good neighborhood once upon a time. Many years ago you had your Irish in there. You had your Jewish people, your Italian. They were family people, and they knew how to work very very hard.

Mama and Dad worked, and so did Granny and Gramps. The kids, they all worked. They shined shoes and delivered newspapers. They took care of little babies, and nobody complained.

Now you get the colored on Welfare. I want this and I want that. Discrimination this and gimme my rights that.

So the windows are all broken, and they take spray paint and write fuck you honky motherfucker on the wall and street. Shoot heroin and smoke crack cocaine, and get guns to shoot their mother with if their mother had her Welfare money.

What do you have to do to get a drink around here? Who do you talk to about that?

I don't know anymore. I used to know.

My own father, he liked to drink.

Try this, he said to me, and slapped the side of my head.

My ear ringing like bells.

Try this, he said, and whacked the other side.

That's a love tap, he said.

You gonna cry now, he said. Little girl gonna cry now. Little pussy.

He had a red face, and his eyes were yellow. He smelled like whiskey, and he squinted and unbuckled his belt.

You want something to cry about, he said. I'll give you something to cry about.

Fucking pansy.

Then he came in much later, and he cried and cried. He lay down on the bed.

Your old dad is a piece of shit, he said.

Dad put his arm around you, and he shook and cried.

All would be quiet after a little while.

Dad loves you very very much. Dad wants you to be strong.

You make your old dad very happy, he said.

Then he lay there, and then he unzipped and said, You make Dad very happy.

He said, Okay, and he put my hand there. Very strange. It did feel hot like a stove, and smooth, and he go up, he go down, then Dad shake all over, and make mess. Squirt on my hand and on his shirt too.

Our secret, Dad said. Me and you and nobody else at all.

He kissed me on the cheek and on the lips. Lips and tongue all wet like spit.

Dad say, I love you, Henry.

He did too, let me say that now. And I cry now when I think of Dad, and he died with the cancer, and left Mama with a stack of bills and many many tears.

MD is almost sweet to the taste. Little air bubbles. Glug, glug.

Television had game shows and news and weather. You want to be with the owl in the forest of the great Northwest, you press the button. You want New York, Broadway and Wall Street, you press the button again. Soccer in Italy, cartoon of blue people.

You name it, you can have what you want.

I loved that boy and I love him to this day. The boy grew up a little bit at a time and I did all that I could. I bought clothes for him.

You want dungarees, you want white sneakers, you want that Indian vest with beads on the pockets? Okay, sure.

Henry loves you with all his heart and with all his soul.

The boy looked at me, I remember. The boy had blue

eyes, and he looked at me, and I said to him, What are you looking at, and he did not even say, Yes, no, maybe.

Not a word.

I stopped the car, in the middle of the hills in the state of Washington, it must have been. The sun shining, and cars going fast as can be. I pull over and stop. I say, Would you like to tell me what your problem is, and he will not tell me.

So get the fuck out, I told him.

He looked at his hands and his feet.

Go ahead, I said. Out.

He sat and sat like some kind of bump on a log, my mother used to say.

Call the cops, I said. You want to lock Henry up. Go ahead. See if I care.

They come up and put the handcuffs on Henry, they take him down to the station, they put his fingers on the ink pad, on piece of paper, they take a picture with a number down on his neck.

They take you too, I told him. You think they won't. Don't be kidding yourself. You go down to the juvenile hall. All the colored boys, they like to see a nice white boy like you.

Hey, white boy. Hey, honky motherfucker.

Go ahead.

Cars went by, and they had tags from all over. From Oregon and Utah. California, Nevada. One tag was from Virginia. We been everywhere, I said to myself. This boy and me have been almost everywhere.

So he sat, and continued to sit, and finally I said, What do you want me to do? You tell me, if you please would.

And then I believe I began to cry, and those were real tears. Those were from the bottom of my heart and my soul.

That boy was a beautiful beautiful boy. That boy had

brown hair and blue eyes, and when he smiled, when I said something funny to him and he smiled like a picture, it was the sun breaking through on a cloudy day, let me tell you.

The boy had freckles on his nose and cheeks and chin, and he smelled like milk and like grass after it is cut, and even when he was sick from something and throwing up and shitting like anything, he was a beautiful beautiful boy.

Lying in bed, under the sheet, his underwear and nothing else, and cold sweat on his forehead, and looking as pale as a person over to intensive care, and those eyes just blazing like fire.

I brought the boy ginger ale for his stomach, and I put a cool cloth on that forehead, and I got a sponge and pulled the sheet down, and I gave the boy a cool sponge bath. Along the white legs and arms. Over his chest and stomach, and down there too, because I took the underwear off him. And it was lying there, quiet in its nest, and I let the water drip on the boy's skin.

Pale pale skin, and the boy hot like fire still, and looking at me all the while. His hands and feet big, and all they were was bones, and then he would feel a little bit better.

The boy would eat crackers, and then he would get up for the bathroom, and later the shower to wash himself and wash his hair. His hair shined and was like silk, and I put my arms around the boy and told him I loved him and I would die if anything would happen to my boy.

Outside, the sign would blink at all hours, and the traffic on the interstate would pass and pass and pass. That would be in Georgia, I believe, and flat as the top of this table.

Across the way they are on the swings and the slide.

They are very little ones, perhaps the first or second grade, and later in the day the older ones will be out. They play kickball, and they yell sometimes at each other. They push a girl, and she falls to the ground, and they need to be spanked. They will do anything they want if you let them. They need someone to take them by the scruff of the neck and show them who is who and what is what.

They put me in Bridgewater one time, and the docs they wanted to know if I was attracted to women. They showed me pictures of them minus their clothes, and they had big ones and that dark in the middle. What do you feel, Henry? they said to me. Does that excite you?

The lady was smiling, and she looked at me.

Then they showed a picture of a boy, with just a little hair and his thing straight out.

Could you tell us how you feel, Henry, and I would take that in my mouth and that boy would be in heaven all at once, but of course I would not say that.

Where do you get a picture like that? I tell them. That is sick. What is wrong with you?

He wrote down on his pad of paper, and he showed me a picture of a dead person, and a picture of a man in a uniform, and a lady with a whip.

All the time at Bridgewater, they rub my arm and say, So you will relax, and then the needle, and I almost fall asleep. I could not talk if I wanted to.

You go all over, and you look for boys, and you will not stop this, the doc said to me.

The court finds, the doc said, and he said there was an operation, and that I would never have to worry again, and then I would be a member of society.

So tell me please, he said.

Then at Walpole, in the Special Unit, there were only seven of us, and the guards were always there, and the other men, in the dining hall and on the way to the infirmary, they said, Hey, Mary. Hey, Michelle.

They said, You fuck little boys.

They said, Hey, Shorteyes, and they would laugh like a hyena.

They let me out because all they had was the pictures of boys in my room, and nothing else, and I was a man of fifty-nine years old with gray hair. I paid my taxes when I had a job.

Work security, work washing dishes, work cleaning up the office when everybody gone home.

They didn't know about the boy, because he grew to big strong young man. He could beat me then with one hand behind his back.

But I love that boy very much, and still to this day.

Can I come with you, mister, he said, because there was something with his mama and dad. They would hit him, and ask him to take his clothes off for pictures. And they died in a car crash.

So sure, I told the boy. Me and him drove here and we drove there. The boy would laugh, and some days he would sing along with the radio, and out the windows of the car we would see the Rocky Mountains and pine trees and deer and elk.

We would stop at nine or ten at night, and we would eat breakfast. Pancakes and French toast, and plenty of maple syrup. Then we would go to the motel, and we would fall on the bed, we were so tired.

That boy had brown hair, and it grew very long in back. Shiny and down to his shoulders. He was thin, and his skin was like nothing I have ever known in my life. It was fresh and it was smooth, and it was like the petal of a flower. So very very beautiful.

I love the boy. I love that boy, I would tell him. I said it to him then. I would say that to him even now.

[16]   He Imagines

The boy was thin, and he had brown hair and blue eyes, and when he was eight years old he read comic books, and watched television, and rode his bicycle around the neighborhood. He liked a girl named Susan Boudreau, who was in his class at school. She sat in the row near the window, and she had curly black hair, and she smiled when Mrs. Stanley, the teacher, called on her.

He read the Hardy Boys books. He read about Frank and Joe Hardy, the boy detectives, and their father, Fenton G. Hardy, who was a world-famous detective. They found treasure in an old water tower at a railroad siding. The man with red hair nearly ran them off the road when they were riding their motorcycles. They found the smugglers' ring in a cave on the side of a cliff. Their Aunt Gertrude made delicious apple pie.

Sometimes he read, lying on his bed, and when he looked up after hours of reading, he was surprised to see that he was in his room, and the sun was shining outside, and nothing in his life had changed.

His brother Jim was three years old, and he walked around the apartment quickly, and once in a while he fell over and began to cry, and the boy would pick him up, and pat him on the back, and say, Okay. Okay. Everything's okay.

Jim had dark hair and eyes, and he always smelled of milk, and was very warm. The boy was amazed at how small Jim's hands and fingers were.

He sometimes wondered what would happen if Mom was hurt or killed, and could no longer take care of him and Jim. He wondered if they would be separated. Maybe Jim would be sent to a family that lived in California, on a farm with horses and orange trees, and there would be three or four other kids, all of them older than Jim, who would become Jim's new brothers and sisters. They would take him fishing, and would teach him to ride a horse, and at night, when they went camping, they would build a small fire to cook on, in a clearing among the pine trees, and after dinner they would tell ghost stories, about the haunted house or the man with the golden arm or the woman who lost her only son at sea, and walked up and down the seashore at dusk each day, wearing a black shawl and waiting for her son to return.

They would be in sleeping bags, in tents, and late at night Jim would wake up and hear a twig snap in the woods. He'd hear what he thought was whispering, but maybe it was just the sound of the wind, or a rabbit or squirrel. He'd see the dark lumps of the other sleeping bags, and then he'd go back to sleep.

The boy thought about what might happen to him. He thought about being adopted by Susan Boudreau's family. She had a brother and sister who were in junior high school, and lived in a brown house near Newtonville Square. He thought about being adopted by a rich man who had white hair and kind gray eyes. The man had lost his own son and his wife in a car crash, and he sat in front of his fireplace each night, and thought of them. But when the boy came to live with the man, the man began to take an interest in life once again.

The boy thought about his own father too. He was the only kid in his class who did not have a father, or who did not know anything about his father.

His mother said only that his father was alive, and loved him very very much, but was sick and could not be with them.

He lived somewhere in Boston, and he was in the hospital much of the time, and the boy wondered what disease he had. If he had cancer or heart disease, or if he was in a wheelchair or an iron lung that had to breathe for him.

Maybe his father was some kind of spy for the government, and was somewhere in Russia or South America. The work he did was so secret that nobody, not even his own wife, could know about it. The boy pictured his father as tall. He would have blue eyes, and when he smiled and patted the boy's head, he would say how sorry he was to have been away for so long. He would bring the boy a souvenir from India or Brazil or China. A knife with a black handle, or firecrackers, or gold coins that had been found in a sunken ship.

Or his father was a famous doctor, who went secretly around the world to treat people who were the presidents of countries, or he was an undercover policeman, or a criminal lawyer like Perry Mason on TV.

The boy had freckles, and he was in the highest reading group at school, and sometimes at night, after the dinner dishes were washed and dried and put away, and after Jim was asleep, and he had changed into his pajamas and brushed his teeth, he would sit on the couch with Mom and she would read to him, or she would tell him stories about when she was a girl.

She grew up, at first, in Dorchester, which was part of Boston, on the third story of a three-story house, a three-decker, she called it. Her Mom and Dad—Gramma and Grandpa—both worked very hard, but they didn't have much money.

That was during the Depression, she said, back in the thirties, when the whole economy collapsed, and people were out of work, and men and women had to stand in long lines to get a cup of soup and a piece of bread, because they were so hungry and had no money to buy food.

It was very cold sometimes in the winter, and she remembered seeing groups of men, some of them wearing rags on their hands for gloves, standing around a fire in a trash barrel, trying to get warm.

Men would sleep in doorways, and under bridges, and on very cold mornings they might be found frozen to death, as cold and hard as an ice cube.

Things were very very bad back then, Mom said.

The boy asked if his father was like that. If he was very poor, and if he sometimes slept in doorways or under bridges.

She said she didn't think so, but she didn't know for sure. She said it was hard to say because she hadn't heard of him in a long time.

Maybe sometimes he did, she said. Maybe he had to.

She said her father used to work as a carpenter when he could find work. And when he couldn't, he would sweep streets, or shovel snow or cut people's lawns in the summer. Sometimes people would pay him with a loaf of bread, or a jar of peas or beans.

Her mother took care of other people's kids, or she cleaned their houses or did laundry. And after a while, things got better. Her father got a job in a factory in Watertown, and her mother was able to stay at home. They rented a house on a lake one summer.

He asked if she thought his Dad would ever come back.

Sometime when he's better? the boy asked.

Mom sighed and looked at him. Then she looked at the window across the room.

I don't want to get your hopes up, she said. It's not likely, I'm afraid. He's very sick, and I don't expect he'll ever get well.

Not even in five years? he asked. Or two years maybe?

She said she couldn't say.

She stood up, and checked the lock on the front door, and shut the lights off in the living room.

Then he was in bed, and his thoughts began to whirl and race. Whenever he was lying in the dark, his brain seemed to start up. He'd see the man who came to visit them years ago. His name was Walter or Wendall. He wore checked shirts, and late at night he sat in the living room, in the dark, his eyes glittering, and when the boy got up to go to the bathroom, the man said, C'mere, and the boy sat on the couch next to him.

The man put his arm around him, and began to talk. His breath smelled like medicine.

He said there were people in the world who wanted to do things to him. They wanted to take eveything he had, which wasn't much, and they wanted to lock him away in a place where all the windows had bars on them, and big men in white walked around, and told him what to do all the time.

Told him when to eat, when to take medicine, when to go to the bathroom, and sleep, and brush his teeth.

But he wasn't going back there, he said. He wasn't having any of that.

He was silent, and the boy didn't know whether to keep still, or get up and go back to bed.

The man lit a cigarette, and in the dark, the flare of the match made the man's face look like the side of a rocky mountain. There were crags and cliffs, and hollow, shiny places.

The head of the cigarette glowed.

They're all crazy in there, the man said. They're all loony as bats, he said.

They walked around in robes and slippers, and some didn't move for weeks, from chairs in front of windows, and some could never sleep.

They did terrible things to themselves. They drank gasoline, or cut themselves with knives or razors. They said their husbands or wives tried to poison them, tried to steal their money, wanted to lock them away forever.

The boy was quiet, and it seemed as though the man had forgotten he was there.

Then they let him out, and he lived in a room, and during the day he went to a clinic. They gave him medicine and money, and at night he went back to the room.

He bought bottles of wine, and he sipped the wine all night long, and had horrible thoughts, thoughts he couldn't stop, thoughts he wished would go away.

Lying in bed, the boy remembered him from all those years ago. Sometimes he thought the man was his father, and sometimes he didn't know. Mom would not say.

But after he left, she began to get fat in the belly, and then Jim came late one night. Grandpa stayed with the boy, and then Mom came back with a white bundle, and Jim was screaming and crying.

The boy turned over in bed, and listened to Jim. Jim slept like stone. He made no noise, and never seemed to move or breathe, and once in a while the boy got up during the night and went to Jim's small bed, the bed with the railing, and made sure he was breathing.

Dana McGrath's father worked for the Post Office, and wore a gray uniform, and one night the boy went with Dana and his father for a ride in the country. On a road somewhere, west of Boston, with trees on each side of the road, and touching overhead, Dana's father shut the car lights off for a moment, and began to laugh, and Dana said, Please, Dad.

He turned the lights back on, and later, they stopped at an ice cream stand, and Dana's father bought them cones. The boy got chocolate.

Susan Boudreau's father worked in Boston for an insurance company, and Mrs. Stanley, the teacher, was married and had a boy and girl of her own, and her husband was a dentist.

Susan's father was short, and he was bald, but he drove a Buick that was as big as a kitchen.

The boy had never seen Mrs. Stanley's husband, but he thought Dr. Stanley wore glasses and a white coat all the time, and he would smell like a dentist's office.

Someday, he would come home from school, and a man would be sitting in a chair in the living room. Mom would be there, and she would be smiling and almost laughing, and Gramma and Grandpa would be sitting on the couch. There were two or three enormous leather suitcases in the corner, and two shopping bags of presents wrapped with bright paper, and Jim would be sitting on Mom's lap.

The man in the suit would stand when the boy came in, and he was tall as the ceiling almost. He smiled, and put his hand out, and said, Son.

Sweetheart, Mom said, and she stood up too, with Jim in her arms, and the man put his arms out, and gathered the boy in.

Or he would be at school, and he would be called down to the principal's office. He'd walk down the shiny, echoing corridors, and he'd pass classrooms where all the students were sitting in neat rows, and he could hear the teacher's voice grow loud just as he passed, then fade as he walked along.

When he reached the office, the secretary smiled at him, and motioned with her arm, and he went to the inner office.

Mom was there, and the principal, and a strange man who wore a brown leather coat, and a white scarf. He had dark hair and blue eyes, and the boy would know, just from looking at him, that he was the one, he was his father.

Or he'd be walking down the street, maybe on his way home from school. It would be April or May, and the sun would be bright and warm. The leaves on the trees and bushes were beginning to bud, and he could hear birds singing.

Then a car would pull up to the curb. A black car, a red car. A man would roll down the window, and the boy would stop. And it would happen like that, almost without movement or words.

They'd look at each other and know. It would all be over.

The man would have brown hair, and green eyes. He'd smile.

[17] Nick

I was a train wreck then. I was hustling on Market Street and South Street. The car'd pull up, windows would roll down, and they'd say, How much?

Depends what you want, I would tell them. You want to fuck me, you want me to suck you? You want a half hour in the front seat of the car? You want me for the night at your apartment? Your hotel room?

They were all kinds too. You'd be surprised. Lawyers in suits, carpenters, construction workers, doctors, one time even a judge. That was at a bar association convention.

Now and then they want you to tie them up and put them in a closet, but leave one hand free so they can jerk off. One kid I know got paid to pee on someone. They got all kinds out there. Things you wouldn't believe.

I could make fifty, eighty, a hundred and a half for the whole night. They buy you dinner, drinks, they want to give you flowers even. You sleep in the big wide bed. Clean sheets, a view out the window of the lights, the harbor.

So the one guy, he pulled up and said, Get in, and he paid the hundred and a half, and he drove around and around. I saw the waterfront, I saw downtown, the expressway, I saw the suburbs. All those lawns, the split levels like on TV.

Talk to me, the man said. Where's your mama and daddy?

He bought a six-pack, and he took one from the ring, and he gave me one. I had pills too, had them in the watch pocket of my jeans. I had Demerol, codeine, Talwin, Valium. I could name all of them now. The book I read was the PDR, the *Physician's Desk Reference.* I knew that book like the preacher knows the Bible.

But all of this was before. This was fourteen, fifteen, sixteen. I could sell a pint of blood, I had to, could get a meal at Sally's for free. But now I'm in the program, and it's not just my body here. First it was, but not anymore.

DSS, social services, said, This boy is out of control, and we feel it is not the fault of the mother, and they were right on that. Mom was at home, Mom had a job, Mom had Caitlin, my sister, in junior high school. On the honor roll. The whole thing.

My dad was long gone, but that was no excuse either.

The court said, You want the youth facility, or you want to go to rehab? Project Phoenix?

It didn't take a genius to figure the program would be better. I had spent a night or two at the lock-up, and it was not a place I cared to go back to. So here I am.

This is not in the city at all. We are twenty miles southeast or so. There are hills here and trees, and plenty of farms. You can look out the second-story windows, and see fields and silos, and tractors moving up and down like ants in the fields. The air is cold, and you can smell cow manure.

There are just eight of us, and there are some stories here. Guys from prison, and guys from the state hospital. I am the only one who was on the streets, although in here they say that I was out in the weeds.

Cheryl is the director, and there are three counselors, and we do the cooking and the cleaning. Ron is my counselor, and we meet for one hour every day. We also meet in group, and we go to AA at night, and in between we smoke butts and study and we think about how we got here, and what it felt like.

Ron said, So you're on your hands and knees on a bed in some hotel room, and some sweaty bastard with money has his dick up your asshole, and he's sliding it in and out, and you're there on your hands and knees?

Ron said, I want you to think about that. I want you to remember what that felt like.

Ron tried to make me cry, and sometimes I had all I could do not to.

He said, What would you do if you had a baby, a child of your own? You raise this baby. You feed him and wash him, and you watch him grow. And then he gets older, and he starts stealing money from your wallet so he can buy pills? He stands outside the liquor store and gets people to buy for him?

And pretty soon he's out on Market Street giving blow jobs and getting fucked in the ass? Is that what you want for your baby? For this kid you raised?

Think about your mother, Ron said. I want you to think about her for me.

I did not look up at Ron. The tears were running down my face.

Ron said, What're you feeling right now? I shook my head.

Talk to me, Nick, he said. He put his hand on my wrist.

Right now, he said, his voice low. What are you feeling?

Nothing, I said.

152

What else?

Nothing at all.

It hurts, he said.

I shook my head.

Will this kill you?

No.

Ron smiled. You've got to think, he said.

He said, I want you to stay with this. I want you to think about being on the streets, and hustling, and getting fucked up on drinking and pills. I want you to remember all of that as best you can.

Where they took you, and what they said, and what they smelled like and looked like. And I want you to remember how you felt through all of this, and how it was when you began to get numb.

Then Ron didn't say anything and I didn't say anything. I could feel his eyes on me, and I thought of the farms and the trees and the sky.

I said, Is it time?

He said it was.

Then I went out and downstairs, and I was inside out, was raw. I was exposed nerves.

I went out on the deck, and smoked, and Stewart was inside vacuuming, and Mike was on the couch writing in his notebook, but they didn't say anything to me.

And I thought of the man who picked me up, and he paid me the hundred and a half up front, and then we drove all over, and he said, Where's your mama and daddy?

He had a beer and I had a beer, and then I took a codeine and a Talwin, and I told him my dad wasn't there. My dad never married my mom, and she wasn't even sure who he was. She thought she knew, but she wasn't absolutely sure. He may have been this scientist from Eugene, and he lived in the house, the Fifth Street house, just the one summer. Or he might have been a doctor. In the late sixties and early seventies things were loose, and the Pill was new, and there were people moving in and out of houses and apartments. The scientist was there for a while, but he wasn't the only one.

So when the men picked me up, and I went with them, I watched their faces. The one with the suit and tie, the reading glasses perched on the end of his nose. He took off his suit jacket and laid it carefully over a chair. Then he looked up suddenly and smiled, and I thought for a minute that I had seen him before, that I knew him from somewhere.

Some of them slept loudly, slept like some busy stove. They snored and moved their arms and legs, trying to get free of the sheets. Then they draped an arm around me, and pulled me close to them. They smelled like sweat and vodka and soap. And outside and down below, even at two or three in the morning, the traffic kept going by, the cabs stalking, the headlights yellow eyes.

The big man wore jeans and a corduroy jacket, and his car was pretty old. It was a Pontiac, and it was dusty and had dings in the front and sides.

There were empty hamburger wrappers in the back seat. There were plastic cups and bottles and cans. There were dirty clothes, and road maps that were creased and tearing from folding and refolding.

He was big, was maybe forty or forty-five years old. Maybe less. His hair was thick and dark, but there were streaks of gray in it too. He had blue eyes, and wore glasses with brown frames. His eyes were big behind the glasses. They were almost sad.

He had been on the road a long time, he said. He was tired. He wished sometimes he could go away somewhere, to a place far away, where nobody knew him and where he didn't know anybody. And he would just sleep and sleep and sleep.

I could sleep a year, he said. I could sleep forever, almost.

Then he looked at me, and he said, What's your name? How old are you? Where's your mama and daddy?

You from around here? he asked.

He drove through neighborhoods in the suburbs. They were quiet in the afternoon.

He said, How many tricks you do in a week?

They like to fuck you from behind? They like you to suck them?

They want you to do it to them?

He went into a park, and pulled up at the edge of a pond. He turned the engine off.

There were willow trees at the edge of the pond. There were glider swings and benches facing the water.

What's your mama like? he asked me.

I said, She's nice.

How old is she?

Thirties. Late thirties.

He looked at the water. Then he said, You're not stupid, you know. A lot of them are brain-dead. You're not.

Then we drove some more. We went near downtown, and parked again, and got out to walk.

He asked if I was hungry.

He said, You look like shit. You're too skinny. What do you eat?

We went to Shoney's, and he said, No fried shit.

He piled my plate at the salad bar with broccoli and lettuce and tomatoes and carrots.

Jesus Christ, he said. Look at you.

You're what? Fifteen? Sixteen?

Then we went into a liquor store and bought a six-pack, and in the car, he gave me one, and he had one.

He said, Your mama know you're out here?

He said, What happened to your dad?

I took a Talwin from the watch pocket of my jeans, and I was quiet, and after a little while I started to itch.

Then it was dark, and he said maybe we could stop at his room.

The building had a broken window, and the hallway on the third floor was long, and the floorboards squeaked. There were televisions on in the rooms we passed. There were game shows and gunshots. The doors were closed, but the televisions were loud.

His room looked out on the dumpster in back. There was a bed and a sink, and a metal chest of drawers.

He took off his jacket, and sat on the bed, his feet up, his back to the headboard. He patted the spot next to him.

The six-pack had two empty rings. I sat on the bed.

He said, You ever been to the Florida Everglades? He said the Everglades covered hundreds of thousands of acres, and there were panthers in them. Pretty soon the panthers would be extinct. There were mosquitos that could kill a cow, they were so fierce.

He said he wanted to go to Ireland someday. He thought of that all the time because he'd seen pictures and done some reading. All those green fields and the stone walls, and the people in the villages walking to Mass on Sunday.

He liked to stop in towns, and go to the libraries, and just sit down with books. He liked to read the *Encyclopaedia Britannica* because everything you could ever want to know was in there.

Someone went by out in the hall. A man seemed to be humming.

You want to read about Martin Luther, you just look up under L, and there he is.

The thing people didn't realize was that there were

millions and billions of people who lived here on earth before we were even born. People who laughed and talked and fell in love, and we didn't even think of them. They lived and then they died, and then they went back into the earth and became dust again.

We sipped beer, and after a while I took another Talwin.

I look up flowers or I look up Iceland, and I read all about them, he said.

He said there was an article about sleep, about what scientists knew and didn't know about sleep. We spend one third of our life sleeping, and we dream all the time, almost, while we're asleep.

He said, You're a nice kid. I like you.

He got up, went to the sink, turned the water on, peed.

He said, I've been to just about every state in the U.S., and there's something unique about every one of them.

Ever been to the Ozark Mountains? Nobody's ever been to the Ozarks, but they're as beautiful as the Tetons.

Then he was quiet a while, and I looked over, and his eyes, behind his glasses, were full. Like he was ready to cry.

He sipped from the can, and stared at the door, and a half hour went by.

I had three or four pills in me by then, and I felt like God.

He put the empty can on the floor next to the bed, and opened another one.

He said, All of it's in there, in those *Britannicas*.

And the tears were running down his face, like there was some flood in his brain.

Everything in the world, he said. All of it.

[18]   Tate

Bad things happened to him. Bad things happened when he was young. Things he would not talk to me about. Not in any detail at least. Things in Massachusetts, near Boston. His mother and brother were killed, his father was never there to begin with, and then a man came along and took him. They drove around together, him and the man. They drove all over the country. They stayed in trailers and camp sites. In hotel rooms, in cabins in the woods, in rooms in rooming houses. They slept in the car sometimes, in the corner of parking lots. They were always going somewhere else. They were always on the way.

Ellis was tall and he had very wide shoulders, and he spoke slowly. His voice was very low, was hushed, and I would lean forward to hear him.

He had blue eyes, and dark hair that fell forward over his eyes, and he wore wire-frame glasses, little round glasses like John Lennon.

He stopped in the middle of sentences, and I said, What, Ellis? And often he would not even hear me.

Ellis, I said again, and then he would look up, and I could tell he had just traveled a thousand miles, he had just crossed a desert of ten or twenty years.

In all, I knew him about four months, from late in June to late in October. And then he was getting very jumpy, he could not sleep at all, and he was off in the distance almost all the time. Staring out windows and staring at the wall, and not able to see or hear anything around him. I knew that something would happen, and then it finally did happen, and afterward it almost made sense to me.

He said he was very very sorry. He said he loved me like no one else, but he had to go. He just had to go, and nothing could stop him.

And I knew that. Like rain was falling or a hurricane was on its way, and there was nothing in the world to do but just wait and hope and let it pass.

He loaded up his car, the old Pontiac. He had three or four brown paper grocery bags. He had a few pairs of pants and some shirts and socks and underwear. He had some books, he had all kinds of road maps, and that was about it. That was the end of Ellis as I knew him.

Now I am here in this apartment on the ground floor. One of two hundred and seventy apartments in Lawn Acres in Clearwater, on the Gulf Coast. We have palm trees and we have the water less than a mile away, and it is always warm. There are breezes off the Gulf, and there are buildings that look out on the water, and there are old couples in running shoes who wheel their grocery carts to the Safeway two blocks up. Couples in their seventies and eighties. Couples with married children in Ohio or Minnesota or New York.

They owned shoe stores or they were tax accountants or they sold insurance or worked for the government in Baltimore. They love Florida because of the sun, and because there is no ice or snow, and there are millions of people like them. People in lemon jogging suits, in running shoes, going on trips to England and South America and the South Seas.

My apartment is quiet. They built everything with walls a foot thick. I have a giant glass sliding door in my living room/dining room. It looks out on the back to other apartments on the right, and to a patch of woods to the left. There is a futon on the floor in the bedroom, a futon couch in the living room, a table and two chairs, a kitchen the size of a bathroom.

The walls are bare. The first time Ellis came in, he said it looked like nobody lived here.

I was in Cleveland for a while and then I was in Seattle, and for a short time, for less than a year, I was in Texas. I think of Cleveland as red brick, and rust, and oil on the lake. I think of Seattle as the Korean grocer on a corner near my apartment, and the sticks and seaweed that washed up on the shore of Puget Sound, and Texas as always late at night, and there are 7-Elevens and hamburger places open all the time, and those sodium streetlights that make everything seem bright and unreal, as though it can't decide if it's midnight or noon or five a.m.

Right away, I liked him. There was something there, in his eyes and voice, in the way he stood. He wasn't like anyone you'd ever known. He had been places and seen things, and that made me think about him.

The first time in bed was very slow and sweet, and then when he couldn't do it, when he just couldn't get aroused like that, I almost liked him even more. He offered to help me get there, but I said it was okay, I didn't mind at all.

So we lay in bed, and the walls were white, and this must have been one or two in the morning, and we started to talk. I told him about Cleveland, and my father and mother, my brother Leo, and my two sisters, Martha and Ruth. I told him about the tire swing in the backyard, the one that hung from the box elder, and how we spent hours on that swing when we were very small. We'd lean back, our faces pointing up toward the leaves and branches, and past that to the sky, and Dad would push, and we'd swing higher and higher. The rope would creak, and the whole world swung, and Martha always began to giggle.

In the fall the leaves turned yellow, and fell to the lawn, and when you looked out the back windows in the fall, it looked like a shower of gold. And then Dad raked them, and Leo helped, and they'd let us run and jump into the pile of leaves. After that Dad burned the leaves, and I still remember those fires. The smell of them, and how my father stood next to the pile, leaning on the rake, wearing a black and red checked hunting shirt.

Where was your mother? Ellis asked, and that startled me, that he would ask. He wanted to know, and it was funny because I knew exactly where she was—inside, making soup. She always made soup on Saturday or Sunday afternoon. Chicken soup or potato soup, with onions and celery and lots of basil and pepper, and often she'd make cornbread too.

And all through the neighborhood, up and down the street, there were kids on bikes, kids jumping rope, fathers raking leaves, or waxing their cars in the driveway. Every house, almost, had three or four or five kids, and as it got later, it got darker, of course, and chillier.

Ellis and I were lying in bed, under a sheet, with no clothes on, and we were holding hands as we talked. I thought, What is this? This is amazing. Because we hadn't done it, hadn't made love and then rolled away from each other and gone to sleep.

He was asking, What about your mother? What'd she do? What was your brother like? What color was the house? And I could feel him there in the dark. Waiting and listening. Wanting to know everything.

Later, I asked him. I said, You tell me. I want to know

every part of your life. Then that quiet, that strange and heavy quiet, settled over him. And I thought, We have a long time. We have forever, if that's how long we'll need.

He moved in after just a week or two. He was over all the time anyway, and there was no sense paying rent on the room he was in. We went over to this big old house with peeling paint, and there were padlocks on every door on the second floor. And it was sad how little he had.

Just a few pairs of pants and socks. Tee shirts, one sweatshirt, a second pair of sneakers. There was a toothbrush in a drinking glass, a trial-size tube of Crest, and two or three books.

We packed all his stuff into four shopping bags in maybe ten minutes. Then he looked one final time through the bureau drawers and in the closet, and then we left.

Sometimes we didn't talk much for days. He had jobs through Manpower and Staffkings, two- or three-day jobs in a warehouse or on a road crew, and I was working for the phone company. So we'd both come in late in the afternoon, would make dinner and watch television. We watched *Jeopardy* almost every night, and it was amazing how many answers he knew. That surprised me, but it shouldn't have. Because the other thing he did was go to the library and take out books, and read them. Hour after hour on the couch in the living room, or lying on the futon in the bedroom. And you could have lit a fire or shot a gun, and I don't think he would have known.

He read books about building the Brooklyn Bridge and about the history of Australia. He read a long book about school busing in Boston, and he read a biography of Lyndon Johnson.

When we were getting ready for bed, we'd start talking. He'd talk about the books he was reading, or I'd tell him about the books I used to read about UFOs. How there were more and more reports of abductions, of people, ordinary people, being taken aboard spaceships.

Most of the time I thought, No. That's crazy. None of it's true.

But then I'd read another book, or see something on TV.

It was always a schoolteacher or an off-duty policeman or a farmer. They'd be out in their car, alone, on some remote stretch of highway. By then, Ellis and I were under the covers, and he'd say, Go on.

And I'd tell him how the farmer would be going along, minding his own business, driving the farm's pickup truck. It was always ten or eleven at night, and he was on his way back from a church meeting or a school board meeting, or from selling some grain in a town ten or twenty or thirty miles away.

He was listening to the radio, and the sky was always clear, and the road empty. There were just fields, and fences, and trees, and there was a near-full moon, and he could almost count the number of cows in a pasture, it was that bright.

Then a light passed overhead, or a series of lights. Something round and huge went directly over his truck, and then maybe a few hundred yards up ahead, it turned so sharply, so quickly and abruptly, that he knew it couldn't be human.

Suddenly his radio and lights and engine went dead, and the truck coasted to a stop. He stepped out of the truck, and the ship was above him, hovering silently, bigger than an ocean liner, and with more lights, and he was being drawn up into the ship in a shaft of white light.

Then things slowed down, and later he had a hard time remembering. There were creatures that were shaped like humans, only they had giant heads, and dark glowing eyes, and tiny mouths.

They pressed something to his stomach, and it stung,

then he was paralyzed, and lying on a table, and they had put something like a wire in his nose and penis and in his foot. The lights were very bright, and there was a humming sound, and there were five or six of them surrounding him.

He saw a pulsing, flashing light, exploding in front of his eyes, and then he was lying on the ground next to his truck and it was colder and quieter. When he looked at his watch, it had stopped at ten twenty-seven, but he knew it was much later.

He drove home, and the clock in the kitchen said four sixteen, and his wife and three kids were all asleep.

The next day, he found tiny scars in his neck and stomach and shin. For days, he wouldn't tell anybody. He was a farmer, and a deacon in his church. He sat on the bank's board of directors, and had once been elected to the county board.

Then he began to have headaches and vague pains in his chest and legs. Dull aches, and burning sensations.

Finally, he told his wife.

Ellis was quiet, and for two or three minutes neither of us said anything.

Then I said, What do you think? And he said he didn't know.

Sometimes, he said, he wondered what had happened, and what he had dreamed.

He thought something was real or that he remembered something, and then he couldn't tell. He just couldn't remember if he was even remembering.

A long time ago, he said, he was in Maine, along the coast, and he was being driven in a car, somewhere along a road. The leaves had already fallen from the trees, and he remembered how they lined the road, all the yellow and red and orange leaves, and they were almost like a carpet or something.

It was raining heavily outside, and the heater in the car didn't work, and he was very very cold.

Then he was burning up, he had a fever and he was sweating, and he remembered that it was night because it was dark. And he thought he was with his mother, and she had put a blanket over him, and she was moving her fingers through his hair.

And then it was very very late, and the sky, in the east, was beginning to turn from black to deep blue, and then to gray, and there were even streaks of red and orange.

He was very warm, he felt like he was burning up. He opened his eyes, and he was in the car, in the front seat, between his mother and a man who had gray hair, and wore glasses and an old wool sweater that smelled like mothballs.

Then he woke up, and he was shivering, and he was still in Maine, and the rain was falling, and it was still dark. And he couldn't tell which thing had happened, and who he had been with. If he had imagined his mother and the man with gray hair, and if he imagined driving in Maine, and the rain was falling, and the leaves were wet on the side of the road.

We were silent a while, and then I could hear him breathe. Then some time passed and Ellis was asleep.

And I think of that now, and where he could have gone to, and what it was like for him. And I start to wonder who he was, and where he came from, and what things happened to him. Because already, this is four years ago, and might almost have happened to someone else, to the person I was back then.

[19]   Medfield State Hospital

Ford liked baseball, and he liked to ride his bicycle all over the streets of Newton, in Massachusetts, outside Boston. He liked to watch television with his mother and brother, with the lights out in the living room, Mom and Jim on the couch, sometimes with a blanket over them, and Ford would lie on the floor, a few pillows from the couch for his head.

Ford liked President Kennedy and his beautiful wife, and he sometimes wondered if his own father, whom he did not think he remembered, looked anything like the President.

He did that when he was riding his bicycle, too. He saw men walking on the sidewalks or driving in cars, and he always wondered if his father had gray hair, if he was short or tall, if he wore a mustache, or dark suits with red ties, green work pants and boots, gray sweatshirts. Did he have a red car? Was he rich or poor? Did he sell Bibles for a living? Did he sell insurance?

Sometimes he thought he remembered his father as a big man with dark hair and glasses, who shaved in the morning in front of the bathroom sink, his face covered with white shaving cream, so that he looked like Santa Claus.

He remembered his father sitting at the kitchen table eating cereal, and he remembered him drinking clear liquid from a glass that smelled funny, and once in a while he would have Ford sit on his lap and he would say to Ford, You love your old man? You love your old dad? And his eyes were red and yellow at the edges, and he smiled, and his lips were wet, and there was saliva, was small white foam like the beach, at the corners of his mouth.

Then he was gone, and Mom said he was not feeling well, and for a long time it was just Ford and Mom on the second floor, and when Mom went to work, Ford went downstairs to Mrs. Tempesta's house, and Mrs. Tempesta made cookies and bread, and she let Ford lick the bowl when she was done with it, and she said he would grow up to be as handsome as John F. Kennedy.

Mrs. Tempesta took out an old cigar box from the top bureau drawer in her bedroom, and she and Ford sat on the edge of her bed, and she showed him pictures.

That's my papa, she said, and there was a man in a dark suit, standing on the side of a hill, and he was not smiling.

That's Lucille, Mrs. Tempesta said, and there was a little girl in a white dress, her hands pressed together like she was praying.

There were pictures of dogs and goats, and there were pictures of people standing next to an old black car, and Mrs. Tempesta said she was four years old when her mama and papa came to this country from Italy.

That was a long long time ago, she said, and her hands went slowly through the pictures in the box, and then she said, Okay, and Ford looked, and there was a girl who was maybe ten, and she had short dark hair, and wore a dress with stripes, and she was squinting in the sunlight in front of a tall house that was half in shadow, and Mrs. Tempesta said, Who do you think that might be?

Ford said he didn't know.

Mrs. Tempesta said, That was me, believe it or not. That was me more than fifty or sixty years ago, and Ford looked at the girl, and tried to see Mrs. Tempesta in the girl, but the longer he looked the harder it was to see.

Then a big man came to live with Ford and his mother, and he was not feeling too good. He had been in the hospital, and then he was staying with friends who were trying to help him straighten out his life. He went every other day to talk to a man who would help him, and he had bottles of medicine lined up on the bureau in Mom's bedroom, and maybe Mom said that the man was Ford's dad, even if he looked different and acted different.

He had been away a long time, and now he and Mom were trying to work things out.

Sometimes Ford heard him crying late at night, and once he got up to go to the bathroom, and Dad was drinking beer and watching television, and he was saying, You don't know even if I tell you, and you pretend to know.

There was nobody in the room with him, and he talked on and on, and when Ford came out of the bathroom Dad was still sitting in front of the television, only by then he was whispering, and it sounded to Ford like air moving inside pipes, at night, when nobody noticed.

Then he was gone away again because he wasn't feeling too good, and Mom's belly began to get big, and she said God was giving her another baby, and pretty soon Ford would have a brother or sister, and then there would be three of them.

In the car, much later, at night, with his face pressed to the window, and staring out at the lights on the sides of the highways—lights way off in the distance, set among dark hills or trees—he wondered who was living in the rooms where the lights were, and he thought about lying in bed years earlier, before anything, and Mom would come in and sit on the side of the bed and say, Honey, say, Ford, and she'd tuck the covers under his chin.

Ford and Henry would get a room somewhere, near the back of the motel where the dumpster was, or they would go to a far corner of a parking lot, at K Mart or at a giant mall, and they had blankets in back, and gloves and hats, which they put on, and they would be quiet a long time, and they could hear the traffic of the highway way far off.

Sometimes late, a car would move slowly through the parking lot, its headlights sweeping the few parked cars, but always they moved past, lighting up, for an instant, the inside of their car.

Once in a while they drove along dirt roads late at night, through woods, or past fields, and sometimes bumps scraped the bottom of the car. Crickets would grow quiet as they passed, but there were other insects clicking and humming in the trees. Once they passed cows in a pasture, and went up a long hill. They passed under trees and power lines, the road became narrower, and Henry drove for a long time, at five or ten miles an hour.

Then he stopped in the middle of the woods, and they were miles from the paved road. Leaves and branches scraped the sides of the car, and when Ford got out to pee, he was surrounded by darkness and bushes. He pushed through, into the woods, and overhead, through the canopy of trees, he could see stars and a quarter moon.

He stopped in a small opening in the underbrush and began to pee, and when he finished he stood for five, for ten minutes, and listened to the insects.

They were in Missouri, and they had been driving for three or four days, with brief stops at the side of the road.

Ford thought he could keep walking. He could walk

through the woods in the direction of the North Star, and cross streams and hills and fields. There would be deer and fox, raccoons, squirrels, and they would be still as he passed.

Sooner or later he would come to a farmhouse, and a white-haired man and woman would be inside, and they would turn when they heard his knock, would go to the door, look out through the curtains, and then smile when they saw his face. Almost as though they knew he would be coming.

Inside was warm, and smelled like coffee and baking bread, and there was a fire in the fireplace. The logs snapped and popped as they burned, and outside Ford could feel the darkness, could hear the insects, loud as an ocean. Then he was back in the car, and sleeping.

I am lying in bed, in here, and they come in with injections every two hours. They touch the spot with cotton and alcohol, and the needle, and I am swimming once again, and everything floats and swirls, and there is an ache in my chest, then it moves to my neck, my legs, my wrists.

Why don't you tell me, Dr. Vaughn says. Why don't you share that with me.

He is bald on top, and grows the hair long on one side and combs it over the bald spot. He looks at me and smiles. He is sad, and nods his head, and his eyes grow large. He smiles again.

Sylvia holds the needle, and says, One sec, and late at night Steve says, Hold on there, and in the evening Bill tells me it's time.

I roll the sleeve up on one arm, the other arm, but after a while both arms ache like someone has been punching them. Then I slide the top of my jeans down two or three inches, and they pop the needle in at the side or back. And I am quiet as a weed in water, as a frond at the bottom of a lake. I wave and sway, and am silent. I can see the surface twenty or thirty feet overhead. Can see the light, and feel the weight of water, and all of it shimmers, and I don't say anything.

There are boys everywhere. A thousand boys marching in a long line across the savannah, in tattered clothes, on legs skinnier than thread. Boys with flies swarming around their eyes and noses and lips. Boys walking together to somewhere else. Away from the big guns, from airplanes that drop bombs. Boys who have not eaten anything but grass, but four or five grains of rice. Boys with eyes the size of ponds. Boys without water, whose lips are white and cracked.

There is a boy in Dallas, Texas, in a room, and he stares around him, and does not move, and for hours he sits on the floor, and still does not move, and his mouth is open, and his breath is rapid, and late in the afternoon, after the light from the window has shifted, has grown bright and high, and later has grown lower and softer—a woman comes in and says, What is wrong with you?

The boy has a blanket, and he looks at her, and he begins to tremble.

Spoiled rotten, she says, and he watches as she moves around the bare room, pacing from side to side. Pacing from the window to the empty closet.

She reaches down and feels the blanket and then his diaper with her hand.

Stinky, she says. Stinky, filthy boy, she says.

You expect me to clean this up, she says.

She picks him up by the diaper and swings him around.

She says, I work all day, and you think I like to come home to this.

There's a girl in Montana in a trailer. A girl with two brothers, with three sisters. Her father is in a wheelchair and her mother is crying at the kitchen table, and there are dirty diapers in the corner. The two babies are crying, and the television is loud.

The girl picks up one of the crying babies, and sings a song about birds and flowers and the ocean.

In Little Rock, Arkansas, Daddy can do that if he wants to. Daddy can whisper to her and make her giggle, and he can tickle her too.

No, Daddy, no, Daddy, she says and laughs, and Mommy will be at the grocery store, and then she will be at the Post Office, and then she will be at the doctor's office with Meredith.

Daddy, do the face, the girl says. Please, Daddy. The face like the gorilla.

He curls his lips and his cheeks puff out, and his shoulders go up to his ears. He makes grunting sounds.

She laughs and shrieks, and he tickles her, and after a while he says, Okay now. Okay now.

Shhh, he says.

Quiet time, honey, he says, and puts his arms around her. He holds her tight on the couch.

Shhh, he says.

And his hands begin to do those things. His hands on her arms and belly. His hands on her back and on her neck, and up and down her legs.

He says, Shhh, honey. Quiet time now.

And he hums. He is warm as a bear, and he hums.

Shhh, sweetie, he whispers. Quiet as a mouse at night, he says. Quiet as a dream.

In Indianapolis, he walks up and down the parking garage at the airport, and he checks the doors of the cars, and on the E Level he finds a back door unlocked. He looks around, sees only darkness and shadows, then gets in the car. He lies down on the back seat, curls up.

He hears airplanes taking off and landing, and hears cars down below on the streets. He hears a siren, hears a car horn, hears a blip like the start of another siren.

They have tattoos in the shower, and they are all wet, and four or five of them surround him, and they are smiling.

One takes his wrist, then another holds his other arm, and he tries to scream. The water is falling, and there is steam, and the rest of the boys do not watch.

First one does it, then another, then another. Four of them do it to him. The water falling, and soap, and steam, and they don't say anything. He can hear their breath get faster and deeper, like they are running a race.

The boy in Newark sleeps in a hallway, under the stairs in back, and snow is falling outside. People go up and down the stairs, every half hour or hour, but the boy does not hear the footsteps.

He is covered by a painter's drop cloths, which smell like paint and turpentine.

The girl in Elkins Park, near Philadelphia, sleeps deeply, and dreams about the summer, and in the dream her father is still alive. He walks toward her from a long way down the beach, and he is wearing shorts and sandals, and a polo shirt that is unbuttoned at the neck. He is tanned, and he has not died, and he is smiling at her.

He forgot things, and wants to tell her. He wants to tell her about when he was a boy all those years ago, and the things he now remembers.

He meant to tell her before, tell her way back then, but it was suddenly too late. He was slipping away.

Mom was there, and Katherine and Andy, but he was going away. The nurse wrapped a blood pressure cuff around his upper arm, and squeezed the black ball, and then it was too late.

How long can I wait? How long can they keep me here? Thirty days? Two months? Half a year?

At dawn the light is deep blue outside, and shadowed,

like a man's face when he has not shaved. Then the light silvers, and someone pads by in the hall.

In the woods, a man is squatting and waiting. He squints, and licks his lips, and scratches a spot on his back. He is slow and patient as a tree. He can wait forever, can wait until God comes back.

Holy Mary, mother of God, pray for us sinners.

Ford used to go to church, and he knew all the prayers. Mom said it was important. God loved him, and it was important to visit God in his house, in church. At night, just before he went to sleep, it was important to talk to God. To thank Him for all his gifts, for His kindness and goodness.

John F. Kennedy was President, and he was born in a house in Brookline, and Brookline was right next to Newton, in Massachusetts. President Kennedy was Irish and Catholic, and Ireland was across the ocean. That was where Ford's people had come from a hundred years ago. All the potatoes were rotting in the ground, and they had nothing to eat, and so they gathered up their things, and rode on a boat, and came to Boston.

President Kennedy had two children who were not much younger than Ford. There was a boy and a girl, and the girl had a pony of her own. Maybe someday, Ford could have a pony of his own. Maybe he could travel to Washington, D.C., our nation's capital, and see the White House, where President Kennedy and all the other Presidents before him lived. President Lincoln and Franklin Roosevelt, and Calvin Coolidge, who wore an Indian headdress and would not say a word.

The light at dawn is blue and silver, and in Nebraska, there was frost on the lawns in towns. Henry said he could go where he wanted, Ellis could come and go as he pleased, because sometimes—and he sighed—Henry just didn't care anymore.

In Montana they walked on a trail in the Tetons, and they talked loud because that would scare the bears away. The trail was called Going to the Sun Road, and they could see for twenty miles, and Henry said he loved this more than anything—the pine trees and the air. They saw deer and badgers, and he said when he was young he liked to take a tent and backpack into the woods in the winter, in two or three feet of snow. He could stay out there a week or more. Hunt squirrel, build a fire, see the stars at night. Almost nothing moved in the woods in winter. The trees sighed a little, and small animals came out at night. But almost nothing else moved.

They sat on a rock in the sunshine, and there was a drop of five hundred feet or more. There was snow on the peaks. Henry ruffled his hair, and said this was how it was supposed to be. Just the two of them, and all this country. You could feel God out there, he said.

Henry tried to take him all over, tried to show him the sights as best he could. And now Ellis was just about as tall as his old pal, Henry, and before long he'd be just as strong too.

It's all that good food, Henry said, and he smiled. All those vegetables, and all the love Henry gave Ellis, and Ellis didn't even appreciate any of it.

One day he'd wake up, Henry would wake up, in the front seat of the car, and he'd turn around and Ellis would be gone, just like that. The back seat would be empty as a shell. There'd be a blanket, a few candy wrappers, an empty can of Pepsi. And nothing else for all Henry's years of trying.

He was what? Fourteen? Fifteen? And growing like a weed. Growing like Jack in the beanstalk.

And I said, That's not true Henry. I wouldn't ever leave you.

Henry loved the boy, just like he said. Henry kissed

him and held him, and did the best he could for him.

Henry didn't kill his Mom and Dad. He didn't kill Jim either.

Henry did the best he could.

In Michigan, in the basement apartment, Henry went away for two or three days. There were pipes in the ceiling, and a baby crying, and the furnace was in the cellar right next door.

Ellis went out and walked all over the city. There were a few hills, and sidewalks with cracks and weeds growing in the cracks. Most of the leaves had fallen, and the wind was cold, and blew the leaves across the streets and sidewalks.

He stopped in a laundromat to get warm, and an old woman glared at him. He went out again to walk, and he began to feel strange, began to feel as though he could just walk away, and go sleep under a highway bridge, or in a garage or toolshed in a backyard. He could get free meals at the Salvation Army, could get a job at a grocery store or maybe shoveling snow.

Henry said a man was fine as long as he was able and willing to work. As long as he had those two things, he would never have anything to worry about.

And believe me, he said. He knew.

Henry grew up in an institution in New York City, he said. First he was in Dorchester with his family, then New York City. So he knew what it was like. He knew the school of hard knocks. So don't go crying to him.

Henry had the scars to prove it.

You ask, and Henry would be happy to tell you.

The light is almost like ice at dawn. The light is blue and silver, and soon they will have another shot for me.

Dr. Vaughn says I can stay as long as I want, if I so wish.

We have plenty of room, he says.

Sometime after Michigan, after the apartment in the basement, he walked away. He looked at Henry, he turned, and he walked away.

Mr. Johnson was President, and the streets were full of fires and sirens and soldiers with guns.

He was taller than Henry, and he walked in the streets in Chicago and Gary and later in Columbus, Ohio. There were students everywhere, and they let him stay in a big house with posters on the walls, and beads on the doorway to the pantry.

Henry could not say anything. Henry watched him walk away like that, watched Ellis as though there was nothing anyone could do.

You work your fingers to the bone, and what does it get you.

Day after day, week after week, year after year.

It was those hippies, and the colored, and those others.

They didn't want to take a bath, and they were too lazy to work.

What was wrong with them?

Footsteps go past, then there's silence, then a door is being unlocked and locked.

He must have stood there on the street outside Chicago. The car parked near the school, and the houses tall and silent, and all the leaves gone from the trees.

I had a shirt and a jacket, jeans, socks, sneakers. I had brown hair and blue eyes.

And Henry stood there like I was stealing his heart, and there was nothing for him to do but stand and watch as the best and only thing in his life walked away.

[20] Walter

Now it is quiet and unhurried. Now my life is like a season of nature. Leaves are falling softly from the trees, and at night the temperature drops down into the thirties, and when I walk the beach near Scituate Lighthouse, the ocean is gray like stone, and does not seem to hold any kind of life.

I build a fire in the wood stove early. First rolled-up newspaper, then small sticks. They build quickly into a blaze, and in five or ten minutes I put the bigger split logs on top. For the rest of the day the fire will burn. Every few hours I check, poke the embers, move the logs around, and occasionally add wood.

The fire is more than enough to keep the first floor warm. By December, we will have to turn the furnace on for a few hours in the evenings, but the stove does most of the work.

Nora keeps the garden, and she bakes, and she belongs to a reading group that meets once a month to discuss a book they have all agreed to read. She works too with a literacy volunteer program in Quincy once a week. She tutors people who have recently arrived from Asia or Eastern Europe or Africa.

They are eager to learn, Nora tells me.

I am good, they write for her in their workbooks. I will be good. I was good.

How much does that apple cost?

It is a nice day.

Do you know the time for me?

Thank you very kindly.

Nora turned seventy in September, and I am three years older than her. She takes a medication for a mild form of arthritis, which is mostly in her hands, and I take pills for my blood pressure.

All six of our children are fine and doing well. Lorrie is in Seattle, and Pete is in Wisconsin. The other four live within a two-hour drive of us. Tim, Jennifer, Steve, and Mark.

I used to say their names to myself in the order in which they were born. Tim, Lorrie, Jennifer, Stephen, Peter, Mark. I did that in the morning when I was waking up, and having my first cup of coffee of the day, and I did it every night, after I shut the light off, and just before I said my prayers.

One Hail Mary, one Act of Contrition, and then one Our Father. When I said the Our Father I always thought of my own father rather than God. I pictured his white hair, and him wearing one of his flannel shirts and work boots. He worked for Edison in Boston, and has been gone now for thirty-three years. I would imagine him in heaven, and I would think as I said the prayer that I was talking to Dad and God. And I always found that soothing and calming all the years I was a cop.

You do that kind of work, and you find yourself thinking of things late at night.

I would say each of my kids' names, then my prayers, and as I was falling asleep, I would remember where each one of them was. Tim in bed, Lorrie and Jennifer in their room, Steve playing hockey at the MDC rink in Brighton—Bill Major's father would drive him home. Pete in bed on the third floor, Mark sleeping over at his friend Brendan Drew's house.

I pictured each one of them, sleeping, or riding in a car. I pictured them under their blankets, the pillows bunched under their heads, or yawning and blinking their eyes the way they did when they were tired.

Nora would already be asleep on her side of the bed, and she would say to me later, during the brightness of the day, Stop worrying, Walter. It doesn't do anyone any good.

For seven years at the end, before I retired, I worked out of the state attorney's office in Government Center downtown. But for most of my career I was at the State Police barracks on Commonwealth Avenue, near Boston University. I worked vice, burglary, narcotics, and homicide, and many things in between. Probably that is why I stayed awake at night, and why now, long after I stopped going to Confession or taking Communion, or even going to Mass most weekends, I never miss saying my prayers before I go to sleep at night.

My grandmother, who came over from County Sligo in her teens, always said you should never go to bed angry or worried about something, and she said the best way to do that was to offer it up to God. Offer the anger, the worry. Say, I have carried this, Lord, all day, and would like to give it into Your hands, and God would always accept.

Offer it up, my grandmother always said when anything went wrong, and my father often said that as well.

Grandma must be dead now fifty years, if that's possible.

Back in the early days, in the days I was starting out, you didn't have to go to college to get on the State Police.

You took a test, and it helped that I was in the Army during the war. Once you were on, you went to the Academy, and after that you took classes at night almost all the time. I finally got my bachelor's degree from B.U. in fifty-seven. Nora and two of the kids saw me graduate.

I got my dectective's badge in fifty-nine.

It is nothing at all like television. There is no resemblance whatsoever. In thirty-one years I never once fired my gun except at the practice range. I never tackled a suspect, or chased anyone in a car at speeds of eighty and ninety miles an hour. It is almost nothing like that at all.

What I did was walk around a crime scene like an archeologist, and notice everything. I knocked on a thousand doors, and asked people if they had heard or seen anything late the night before. I interviewed the husband or wife of the victim, his brother or son or mother, the guy who owed him twenty-five dollars.

What I did was stand around at the Medical Examiner's, watching autopsies, and asking about lividity or hesitation cuts or the temperature of the victim's liver.

Was the bruise on the back of the head from a weapon or a fall? What killed her? The ligature or the stab wounds? Was he drunk when he died? Did he have a full stomach? Was his last meal pizza? Chinese? Chicken pot pie?

Much of it had to do with writing long reports, and with bringing people to Commonwealth Avenue and asking hours of questions. I spent forever on the phone asking questions, and arguing with prosecutors, and sitting with the guys from my squad in bars in Kenmore Square.

The worst cases were the ones involving women and kids, and usually the two would go together. If someone hurt a kid, it would almost destroy the mother. If a mother was hurt or killed, the kid suffered. We worked those cases hard, really hard. They were the ones I tried not to

think about before I was going to sleep, the ones I offered up.

The one in the fall of sixty-three was like that, and I
remember it happened right before Jack Kennedy was
shot. Maybe two or three weeks before.

The call came in from the Newton Police that a boy
was missing, a nine-year-old boy, as I recall. The mother
was a taxpayer, was raising the missing boy and a brother
on her own. She worked as a teller in a bank in Newton,
and lived on the second floor of a two-family near
Newtonville Square.

All they had was that the boy's bicycle was found behind Woolworth's in Newtonville, locked to a fence. He
had come home from school, changed into blue jeans and
sneakers, and then went off on his bike.

There was a father, but the mother had had little con-
tact with him. He had a bad alcohol problem, and vari-
ous psychiatric problems, and he was pretty much out of
the picture.

There was a bad feeling about this one, almost from
the start. We sent someone to check out the father, which
would always be the first avenue, and after checking
through D.S.S., the Department of Social Services records,
we found an address in East Boston, in a rooming house
over near the airport.

Leahy went to see him, I recall, and said, Forget it.
He was in a single rented room, with a hotplate and a
shared bathroom down the hall. His clothes were too big
for him, and he wasn't too sure at first that he even had a
son.

Leahy said his eyes were yellow, and his hands
trembled, and there were empty pint bottles of wine lined
up behind the door. Leahy said he couldn't have taken
himself down to the local store, never mind taking a kid.

The father said he couldn't remember when he had

last seen his son. He didn't seem to know that he had a second son, and he didn't know of course what could have happened to the older one.

The mother was a different story entirely, and when I went out to Newton to talk to her, I began to have that sinking feeling that all of us dread.

Newton is a nice city, a near-in suburb, maybe a ten-minute drive from downtown Boston. It has a reputation of being a rich city, a city of doctors and lawyers and college professors. There are big old Victorian houses, and English Tudor houses, and all of them seem to have plenty of lawn. You go to Chestnut Hill or West Newton Hill or Waban, which are all parts of Newton, and the houses take your breath away, especially if you grew up in Dorchester, as I did.

Other parts of Newton are still nice, but much less wealthy. Parts of Newtonville, or Newton Corner or Nonantum. There will still be trees and some lawn, but the houses are much closer together, and there are some two-families. No three-deckers like in Dorchester, but definitely not Waban either.

The mother lived on the second floor with her two boys, Ford and James. Ford was nine, and James was four or five years younger.

She was very attractive, very neat. She had on a skirt and sweater, and she had brown hair, and I don't think she wore makeup. She couldn't have been thirty years old.

The apartment was a living room, dining room, kitchen, and two bedrooms. One for her, of course, and one that the boys shared.

She said how Ford was a careful and sensible kid. She was always telling him to be careful, and to look both ways before he crossed the street, and to brush his teeth and say his prayers.

His father was gone, she said. His father had terrible problems, had troubles with drinking and mental illness, and because of that, because Ford didn't have a father, for all intents and purposes, she felt he had to be even more careful because there was one less person to look out for him and to protect him.

And she would say that to the boy. She would tell him outright.

And Ford was responsible too. He was such a good kid. He was grown up and serious beyond his years, she said.

I asked what had happened. I asked when she knew he was missing, and if anything out of the ordinary had occurred lately.

She looked puzzled, and I said, Any strange cars parked on the street. A strange man, an unknown man, sitting behind the wheel. Any strangers in the neighborhood.

She shook her head as I talked. She kept blinking her eyes, and once she made a strange sound, almost like a shout or a cry, only she stopped herself before it could get fully out. The sound she did make was like something being strangled.

Did Ford mention seeing anything unusual? On the way to school? At a park or on the playground?

She continued to shake her head.

Did he mention anyone coming up to him and talking to him? Asking him questions? Offering him a ride? Offering to show him pictures or buy him ice cream or candy or something?

No. Nothing, she said. Not that I know of.

She began to sob as I was writing into my notebook. She cried quietly, and said she was sorry, and I waited.

Then she got control, and touched at her eyes with a tissue.

I sat and didn't say anything for a minute or two more. Then I said, Are you okay?

She nodded, and I said, We'll do everything that we possibly can. We have a description of Ford out, and we have our people looking, and we'll do our very very best.

She kept her eyes down on her lap, and she held the tissue in her hand.

Can you tell me about yesterday? About Friday? I asked.

She said she had not gone to work Friday. She just hadn't felt very well. She felt like she was getting some kind of virus or infection, and that was unusual. She almost never got sick, and she almost never missed work either. So Jim stayed with her rather than the babysitter. And around three, three-fifteen, Ford came in, changed into play clothes, and went out on his bike.

Where did he usually ride? I asked.

Just around. Newtonville, through the parks, nowhere very far.

Then I asked to see his room, and like everything else, it was very neat, very clean.

There were bunkbeds, two small bureaus, a picture of Carl Yastrzemski on the wall, a few books, a small desk under the window. There were socks and underwear in the drawers, a few shirts, pants. There were some chestnuts in the bottom of one drawer.

Then she gave me a picture, and he was smiling. He had brown hair, blue eyes, freckles. He was wearing a grey cardigan.

We gave information and a copy of the photo to the *Globe*, and they got it in the paper the next day. And we got calls. People thought they saw the boy—in Connecticut, down on the Cape, in Rhode Island, on the beach in Manchester on the North Shore. One lady said she saw him with a priest, and someone said he saw the boy in a dream. We sent Leahy to talk to a waitress in Maine, and we sent someone to Lawrence to talk to a guy who had been released from Walpole, from the sex unit there, only a week or two earlier.

All the time I thought, we'll get a call about a body in the woods somewhere, or in the weeds in a pond. The body would have been there weeks or months, and we'd have to use dental charts for an ID.

But nothing ever came in, and a case like that has to make you wonder. I don't know what happened to the mother or the brother. I don't know what happened to the father, though you would have to imagine he is dead, particularly the way he was going.

Then Jack Kennedy was shot, and that was pretty bad for everybody, especially if you were Irish and Catholic and from Boston. I remember the horse with no rider during the funeral, and the boot in the stirrup, pointing backwards. I remember, for some reason, that the horse was very old, and was named Blackjack, I believe.

Strange, after all these years, the things that stick with you.

It's cold out tonight. I can feel it at the edges of the windows. The television said it may dip down into the upper twenties overnight. I listen real close, but it's silence everywhere.

Nora's upstairs in bed, probably long since asleep by now. Lorrie's in Seattle, Pete is in his house in Madison, Wisconsin. Tim is in Foxborough, and Jennifer and Steve both live in Weston. Mark lives in Dublin, New Hampshire, just across the state line from Massachusetts. He's on a business trip to Chicago. He'll be home by Friday.

[21]   George

My sister Karen, she said, You fuck up on me you'll go to the youth facility down by Bakersfield, and I don't want another word outa your lying fucking mouth. Donald, her no-good husband, he had already left and gone, and the two squirts were screaming with their diapers full of piss and shit, and the temperature was eighty-seven degrees at nine a.m. already, and Karen had her first cold beer cracked open already and a cigarette in her mouth with the long ash ready to fall any minute.

I said to the judge, I'm fourteen, and know what's up, and they sent me to the youth facility, and I'm here now, and the man with the gray beard, with Coke bottle eyes, he says, Why're you fucking this big guy? Why you giving him blow jobs for ten dollars? There something wrong with you? You don't like girls?

And I say, Sure I suck him and he shoots my mouth full of his come, but it don't taste or smell rotten, and he come by the canal and sit, and he smiled over at me, and Fresno was hot as a cooked chicken in July, and that was the last summer I spent there. And he's really not a bad guy, like to fuck me in the behind. Use Vaseline, and kiss me, and sure I get a little hard. And he liked to suck me a little, and lick around my balls.

Karen's drunk all day and night. Donald come back and bang on the door for hours and hours. Let me in, Karen, he says. I love you, honey, he says and cried like his momma died. One, two o'clock in the morning, and I'm sleeping on the couch, the foam and springs sticking through.

Honey. Karen, I love you, he says, and he loves the little babies with their diapers full, and he's drunk, and next door they're yelling Shaddup, drunken fuck, you, and Karen let him in. He was on his knees, saying, You marry me, and Karen Karen Karen, he was saying, and she's in a tee shirt and nothing but, you see her tits and pretty soon he's kissing and sucking her tits, and she's saying, Oooo oh, moaning like a dog.

I say, Judge, they're all fucked up on beer and wine. They take pills, got dishes in sink and roaches all over.

Fresno's a big diaper full of number one and number two, I tell him. No offense, your honor. You ask me, judge, I tell you. And the judge, he sent me here, to this facility for youthful offenders.

So I was out with Bone, with Billy T, and we were sipping wine in the park near Ventura and Braley Canal, and Billy T says, Fuck you, George, you faggot. They suck your cock, and we slap each other. Him, me, him. I slapped hard, and his nose was bleeding like a cat hit by a car. Bone says, George kicked your ass, and a college boy goes by, and a gray-haired lady. They look at us like we're dirty scum. Why don't you take a shower, why not? they would say.

The canal floats by—paper floats, and wrappers and carrot and onion floats. Scum all over, like me. Scum floating.

Bone wants to go to near the college, where summer girls, they walk with no bras and leave curtains open when it gets dark. So hot, and they take their clothes off. Bone in bushes, he beats off when he see the girl's bush, her tits.

I say, not me, and Billy T, his nose is not bleeding no more, he says go watch college girl naked, no curtain. And you go, you go, I say. I sip this pint of MD and I'll be fine.

Hot as a chicken on a grill, in a cooker. All sweaty, and the big man comes along, he sits on the grass and smiles and says, What're you doing? You drinking your wine? You looking around on this fine hot night?

He calls me, George. I tell him that's my name. Ma and Pa, they're dead many years now. They died in their own puke. Fell down drunk, and puked and can't breathe no more. And Pa shot heroin. Had tattoos all up and down his arms. A scab and snake and dagger.

Pearl, it said on his arm.

The man says he's Ellis now, and he's from way far away, like the Atlantic Ocean, near merry old England, only New England, not the old one.

He stays in a room by the convention center, and he looks around and likes what he sees. Not cold like in Boston and New York City. The big old rotten apple to the core. Tall building like TV. Very nice but very cold. Ice cube.

You want some smokes? he says. He smokes Kools. Wears glasses and he's a big man. Size of cop, only he's nice like a teacher at school. Talks and says many things. I tell how Karen watches TV and drinks Miller beer and Budweiser beer and Coors especially. Silver Bullet, and Karen cries and says, that fucking asshole, Donald, and cries and has a runny nose.

I say sometime I sleep under the porch in back. It smells of wet leaves and cardboard, but Karen doesn't blast the TV there and Donald comes and screams and sucks her tits while I'm trying to sleep there. Moan, oooo oh, and they pull down zippers and their breath is heavy like they're running. Fuck me, fuck me, you big hard dick, fuck me.

I say to him, Mister, you say what you want, I'll do it. You pay ten, twenty dollars.

He says, How old?

I'm honest with you, I'm fourteen in April, and I got very little hair down there. Nothing too proud, but I'm not all boy either.

The sky is mostly dark, and he says where you sleeping, and I say on the couch or under the porch, on the floor in the room with the squirts. Like a closet, and I smell piss and shit. They scream. The baby is four years old and his diaper is full of piss that smells and smells.

I go to school sometimes, but not in the summer, and I steal this, I steal that. Not much. To get this and that.

He put his hand on my arm and moved up down, up down, soft like cat fur, and he says he likes me. He says, you're a very pretty young man, and wants me to stay with him. Two, three weeks. He'll clean me up. I don't mind. Nice bath, and he gets me a clean shirt.

He says he'd like to do that, I don't mind, and Billy T and Bone are gone, and Karen says she'll call the cop and he uses a billy club, and knock my lying stealing face from here to when.

You do it, you fucking cunt, I tell her. You fucking slut and drunk, and she banged my ear with her fist. It rings and rings, and little birds fly around my head like a cartoon on TV almost.

I'm in here, in the youth home, and Randy will be sixteen, he's in the next room. Randy says, so what if he fucked you and sucked you. So who cares? Your sister want to fuck you suck you for twenty dollars? She says to you, I give you all the money you want?

Her check comes and her food stamps, and she takes a shower. Drip drip and rust and roaches all over the shower, and next door they scream that they'll cut your fucking head off, they'll cut your balls off, you fucking cockroach. Karen comes out, and she's wearing her new pants and shirt. She's pretty. She's not drunk, and talks to the lady who comes.

The briefcase lady, says yes, my future, my plans to action. To make my life something good and worthwhile. Not depend on welfare all the while, and have self-respect.

Karen she cries and says she tries so hard and Donald, he bangs on the door drunk as a skunk and he won't leave. And she doesn't say how she moans and he sucks her tits.

And the man in the room is big and moves kind of weird. Says tie you up and put oil all over you and I say I don't know about that.

It won't hurt. I tie you, and you get hard and I get hard, and it'll be fun for all. And he ties me and oils up, it smells like flowers, and he takes a long thing from a bag, a dick of plastic and I say no no no, and I say I'll scream if you touch me, and he says fifty, I'll give you fifty.

Okay fifty, I say, and that hurt that thing, a little. Not too much.

The room has a picture of a cow and tree and lake, and he's red all over, and he asks, you feel good, you like that very much?

We do pills, we do a little sniff, sip wine from a bottle. The radio plays love me love me love me, oh baby, love me all the time.

The wind is in the curtain, and it puffs puffs like a sail on TV. He says, What do you like, pretty fellow? What do you like and want to eat?

I tell him, I want food, and not shit like Karen makes. No cans of stew, no macaroni and cheese. It's yellow like glue. Sticks your mouth shut.

He says, You tell me, I get it for you.

I get Micky D, and fries and big coke, extra sugar in it. I get apple pie, I get a Snickers bar, a Hershey with almonds, I get Twinkies and Hohos.

The bottle is MD, and is full. He says he likes it. He laughs, says all your teeth rot out. You'll have no teeth.

Fuck you, old man, you fucked me just fine, fat old man, and he looks like he's ready to cry.

You're not fat, not really, I say to him. Just big, and okay all over.

Cops go by outside. Lights flash flash flash. Red, blue, red, blue. They scream fuck fuck out on the sidewalk. Smash bottles, scream fuck you fuck you. Police flash by, loud wuh wuh wuh.

He puts my toe in his mouth, says they're candy. Fine with me. Bugs Bunny's on TV, and Road Runner, and Elmer Fudd. A big gun goes boom, and blasts in the mouth. Bombs like bowling balls. Bugs Bunny is black like a colored man, and smoking.

He says, Beep Beep, and runs fast like a car chase, cops going wuh wuh.

Man says a man took him somewhere, he was not even my age then. He says, man said, Get in and you won't get hurt. He fucked him for two days. Tied him up and fucked him, sucked him, every hole he got. He said his ma and pa die. In the ocean or in a car, and the man came.

Big Ellis, he's called.

He moves his hand nice on my arm and back. He says pretty pretty pretty. Beautiful skin, he says. Flower petal.

Bugs on TV wants a carrot, and Elmer Fudd has a cannon to point. Bugs is on a wall, Elmer shoots, and the bomb goes in a circle and blows off Elmer's head.

How are you so sweet, he says. You're a lollypop and honey. You're sugar from Snickers bar. It gives you strength.

You live with me, he says. I'll love you best. I'll love you like you never been loved before. You're like a lollypop, he says.

We'll drive all over, he says. We'll go to the Grand Canyon and Yosemite and see the ocean and white sails.

We'll go in a plane, and see castles and princes.

He says he'll put a dress on me. Ruffles from toes to top, and he rubs my back and says, You're so beautiful. I think I love you, sugar George.

He says he'll treat me good. Not like Karen, and no kids screaming all night, all day and all the time.

He gets a plastic bag out, and gets weed, and lights it and says good weed from Mexico and south down there.

They sell dolls for Barbie and Ninja and for rockets on TV. A boy on TV says, Neat and Cool. Says, Mom, I'll fly a rocket to the moon and down a sewer under the street all the time.

The man likes pills, you feel no pain, no hurt anytime. Can light a match on your finger, no pain forever.

Then it's quiet and cars pass out on the street, and fifty-three channels, and baseball bats, and throws home.

Man on TV said, God and his love and his mercy is good. He looks at me.

Randy in here says all that is shit, and so who cares. They come, they go, and fuck them here, go there. Randy has a tattoo on his hand that says BAD, and he was in a home in LA, he lit matches and almost burned the home down. He says, a needle takes you to heaven and the moon. Maybe to stars, in the sky high above.

Karen says she loves me bunches, and Ma and Pa, they're in heaven now, but they love me. She wants me to light a smoke for her. She says Ma always loved me more and more, and Pa had a monkey on his back. Would never let him alone forever. The heroin.

Pa was in the joint, behind bars, behind fences and glass walls. Go visit Pa in prison. Picks up the phone, says he loves Ma, he loves Karen, he loves George, his baby boy.

Ma gives him smokes and puts her lips to the glass. Pa's face is flat on the glass. Kiss kiss. Karen puts her lips to the glass, George does too.

We have love all around us, Pa says. He says they take everything from us, but we still have more love to fill the whole world. To fill the moon and sea, Pa says. He says he'll come out of jail, he's gonna get us a good house and dog and a horse for Karen.

You like that, he says. You like a house and big car, he'll get it for us. Love takes care of all things.

The screw says it's time now. You go. And Pa tells him two minutes, no shit. He puts his lips to the glass, says mmm mmm like candy, he cries, says he loves us all, more than the world.

And Ma, many years ago she died, gone for all the world and the deep blue ocean. So I go back with Karen or to a foster home.

They say in the home, God loves you, George, and you steal dollars and steal your new sister's piggy bank. They say that hurts them more than it hurts me. They say you want to go to a home where there are bars, to a youth facility. And they send me there.

Man says, You drive for a million miles and you're still not done.

He says please turn the sound down, and sirens go wuh wuh and the man on TV says second down and seven, and a man kisses a lady on TV, and the lady smiles.

Karen says Pa will get out and she'll get a pony, George will get a dog, Ma gets a house, gets a big car. It'll be worth the wait, and pain.

Ma says there's doubt and pain all the time.

The man breathes deep and he'll love me love me love me forever. He says don't leave me.

Twinkies have cream in the center, and my mouth is dry like a cotton ball. He goes grrr like purring on a cat.

He says he'll love and do right by me.

How long, Pa, Ma said. Pa said, as soon as possible. Maybe six months, maybe a year or two.

Karen says Donald is good except when he's drunk. She says, Donald Duck, and he laughs. Donald Trump, she says. He's a nice man with a plane full of dollar bills and a big house.

Vanna, she smiles, she claps. Pat says you spin, and clap clap. Washer dryer, trip to Paris, to New York City, home of the Four Seasons Restaurant.

The man says he'll keep me love me hold me.

I love you George I do, he says. Most sweet, beautiful boy, he says. So I wait, and the cop comes to me on Ventura, she says you punk you little shit. Where's your ma and pa, and you've got no respect for the law, and what's wrong with you.

Karen cries. She says she did all she can, her hands are full, her hands are tied, she can't do what she'd like to do.

Your ma, your pa. They died of drugs. They went to prison, and the kids on the streets, they go along okay.

You'll be a ward of the state, and be in a home with respect and dignity for all and everyone.

He fucks you behind, fucks you in the face, gives you fifty dollars.

In the facility here, a man says, You like girls? The man wears glasses, he says, You like boys better?

Your ma, your pa. Your sister. They love you, but they had problems of their own. They say in Fresno, California, you can have a beautiful life.

Randy says we'll be in here now, then we'll be out. We'll get twenty, fifty, even a hundred dollars. We'll do what we do. Okay, he says.

[22]   He Imagines

The boy rode his bicycle to Newtonville Square, and the leaves were the color of fire. The leaves rose and fell as he rode past them, and skittered over the pavement, and he felt the wind on his face and hands and hair.

In the Square the traffic was heavy. The two parking lots near the Star Market were nearly full, and the traffic on the Massachusetts Turnpike, when he crossed over it on the bridge, was dense but still moving quickly. The high school kids were streaming down Walnut Street, on their way home or to jobs, and many of them had taken their jackets off and slung them over their shoulders. Near the sub shop, a boy and girl were holding hands as they walked.

The boy rode from the bridge at Washington and Walnut Streets, past the banks and drugstores, to the block where the stores ended, at the library. Then he went left, then left again, through a long alley that went behind the stores.

There was a fence in back of the Woolworth's block, and a dumpster, and he got off and walked his bike. There was a big fan going, over a door at the back of a restaurant, and the air smelled like dishwater. He heard dishes and cups and glasses clatter, he heard silverware in trays. Directly behind Woolworth's he locked his bicycle to the chain link fence. He went in the back entrance to Woolworth's, past the restrooms, and down a narrow hallway. Then he was in the Pets section.

He looked at puppies and kittens in their cages, and then he watched three tanks of tropical fish. The fish were bright, and swam slowly past fronds, and through a sunken sea castle at the bottom of one tank. One had a tail as long as the train on a wedding dress, and bubbles rose slowly to the surface.

He went from Pets to Sports. He picked up a basketball signed by Bob Cousy, and it seemed almost to float in his hands. Then he tried on a few baseball gloves. They smelled of leather, and he punched his fist into the pocket of one glove. He thought about the spring, and how he would try out again for Little League, and he thought of how cold it was in April, early in the morning, down at Albermarle. Standing in left field, and waiting for someone to hit the ball, and the sun was hardly over the tops of the trees yet. He had had to put his hand, the one without the glove, into his jeans pocket. Then a coach yelled, Get your hand out of your pocket, left field. Look lively.

He walked past Housewares and Apparel, and in Stationery a woman in a red smock asked if she could help him.

No thanks, he said, and walked past the cash registers, and through the doors. Walnut Street was still crowded. People were moving quickly past—some high school kids, a woman pushing a baby carriage, two old women with gray hair, and kerchiefs tied over their heads.

The boy sat down on the stone wall in front of a church. He watched people cross the bridge, and heard cars go past down on the Pike. Then he seemed to feel something behind him.

He turned, and there was a man lying on the grass. The man had brown hair, and he was watching the people and the traffic going by. He looked at the boy for a moment, then looked away.

The man wore a yellow golf jacket, and dark pants, and when the boy turned around again, he felt the man's eyes.

Excuse me, the man said.

Are you from around here? the man asked.

The boy nodded.

I'm from out west, the man said, and I'm trying to find my way to Concord, to visit my sister and her husband and their kids, and I seem to be lost.

The boy watched the man's face. His teeth were white and his lips thin, and he smiled when he finished talking.

Could you help me? the man asked.

The boy shook his head.

You can't help a poor lost stranger? the man said.

The boy stood up, and went fast toward Woolworth's, and he looked over his shoulder once. The man was still on the grass in front of the church and he was smiling.

The boy began to jog. He ran past a man in a suit, and around a fat man who was getting out of a parked car. The boy went between two parked cars, looked both ways, then ran across to the far side of Walnut Street. He ran down an alley between a bank and a clothes store, and then he was in the big parking lot near the Star Market.

There were people everywhere. People walking and driving in cars, people going in and out of the Star.

He ran between cars, and when he looked over his shoulder, there was no man in a yellow jacket. He ran to Lowell Avenue, went left, ran one block, then went left again.

He was out of the Square by then, and was going past houses, and through fallen leaves.

Ahead, he could see the Newtonville Library, and when he reached Walnut Street, he went down the alley behind Woolworth's. His bike was still there.

He unlocked the bike, got on, and he kept thinking the man was behind him. His foot slipped on a pedal, and he almost fell.

Then he was on Walnut, and he crossed over to the far side of the street, to the side away from the church. He pedaled hard, and when he looked over, there was nobody on the grass in front of the church.

When he reached his own street, the sun was still warm and the leaves still in flame, and he remembered again that it was Friday, and he didn't have to go to school for almost three days. His heart was still beating fast, but he felt better.

His house was one block down, and he could see the tree in front, and the brown peak of the house. He pulled into the driveway, and rode all the way into the garage.

He almost jumped. He turned quickly to the corner behind him, but it was still crowded with rakes and shovels and the trash barrels. There was nobody in the corner.

Mom was in the kitchen, cooking dinner. She asked if he'd had a nice ride, and he nodded. She was chopping carrots and onions and celery for soup. A big pot of water was simmering on the stove.

Nana's coming for dinner, Mom said. She's bringing dessert, and afterward we were thinking we could play Monopoly or do a jigsaw puzzle. And then she's spending the night.

He nodded.

His little brother, Jim, was in the living room watching television. The Three Stooges were being chased through a haunted house by a giant man with an ax. Larry hid behind a door, and when the giant came through, Larry hit him over the head with a crowbar. Then Moe came through, and Larry hit Moe over the head.

Moe hit Larry, and when Curley came through the door, the giant grabbed him. Curley kicked the giant, and all three of them, Moe, Larry and Curley, began to run again.

Jim was lying on the floor on his stomach in front of the television. When a commercial came on, he said, Nana's coming over.

A boy was running down the street on TV in his P.F. Flyers. He could run faster and jump higher, and already, the man in front of the church seemed to have come from a long time ago.

Nana was short, and had gray hair, and glasses so thick they made her look like an insect. She and Mom sat at the kitchen table, and the boy sat on a chair near the stove. Nana and Mom both sipped from glasses of beer. Jim was in the bathroom, washing up.

Mom said she hadn't been feeling well, hadn't been feeling quite up to par, up to snuff.

Imagine, Nana said.

Mom had some kind of bug, some sort of twenty-four-hour intestinal flu that started Thursday evening. She was in on the couch, and this weird feeling went through her stomach, went through her down there.

Sweetie, Nana said, turning to the boy. Why don't you get yourself some ginger ale. I brought some nice Canada Dry. It's in the icebox.

The boy stood up, got a glass, and took the ginger ale from the refrigerator. When he poured, the bubbles tickled his hand and face.

So I called in, Mom said, and all morning, I just stayed in bed, and sort of went in and out of sleep—you know how you do—and had these very strange dreams.

Jim came out of the bathroom, his hair wet, the front of his shirt spotted with water, and when he saw the bottle of ginger ale, he said, Can I've some?

He found a glass, and poured, and Mom said it was very strange sometimes, the things you could think of, especially when you weren't feeling too well, and you'd had too much or too little sleep. Say it was late at night, or very early in the morning. Or if you were home alone, and you weren't used to that.

Nana said she had trouble sleeping at night, and she always thought of John, her husband and Mom's father, and—turning to the two boys—your grandfather, God bless him. He'd been gone now—what was it—seven, eight years, and she still thought of him at least once, every single day of the week.

Mom stood up and took plates and bowls and silverware, and began to set the table, and Nana started to stand up.

No, Mom said, and put her hand on Nana's shoulder. You're fine.

The soup was simmering on the stove, and cornbread was baking in the oven. Mom put butter on the table, and then she opened the oven door, and took out the cornbread.

Nana said she thought of when they first met, when they were just teenagers, believe it or not. Nana's best friend's name was Pearl, and Pearl lived next door to John, and Nana met him on the street in front of Pearl's house.

He was handsome, Nana said. Handsome as John Garfield, she said, and if you have to ask me who he was, well, just never mind.

They went to Nantasket Beach, which was a nice beach in those days, not like it is now, and they walked in the sand and collected shells, and he was a gentleman, a real gentleman. Then they came back late in the afternoon, tired and a little sunburned, and they sat on the front porch at Nana's house, and Nana's mother came out and sat with them for a time, and John was as nice and polite as you could be.

Mom ladled the soup out, and they pulled their chairs up around the table. Mom sliced cornbread, and then she sat down too.

Mom said she wished she could remember something like that, and her oldest son asked what she meant.

I made mistakes, honey, she said. I was young and dumb.

The important thing is that we can all be together here now, Nana said.

What's that mean? Jim asked, and Mom said it meant they were very happy and lucky to have each other.

How did Grandpa die? Jim asked, and Nana said he had problems with his heart, and one morning he just didn't wake up from sleep.

He was dead, right there next to you? the boy asked.

Nana said, Yes. She said it was a shock, because she had gotten up already, and made coffee, and when she came back to the bedroom to shake her husband awake, he didn't move, of course, and she knew something was terribly wrong.

She called the ambulance, and they said right away that he was gone, and then the police came, and then everything else.

What else? the boy asked, and Mom said, Honey. Please. We're eating.

Everyone ate a few spoonfuls of soup, and some cornbread, and the two boys sipped ginger ale.

Then Nana said it really wasn't so bad as it sounded. She said if you had to go, then dying at home in your own bed wasn't a bad way at all. Dying in your sleep, with your wife at your side, was a pretty good way to go.

She ate some more soup, and nobody said anything for a while. The traffic was going past out on California Street, and the refrigerator was humming.

Nana asked if anyone would care for a brownie, and Jim said he would.

After they finished cleaning up, and Jim was getting ready for bed, Nana said maybe they could play a game of Monopoly. Mom helped Jim in the bathroom, and Nana and the boy sat in the living room. He would be the race car, Nana would be the shoe, and Mom, after she got Jim to bed, would be the hat.

Jim came in to kiss Nana goodnight, and then they heard Mom reading to him in the boys' bedroom.

And over and beyond and past anything, Mom read, and then they heard Jim's voice, but they couldn't quite make out what he was saying.

Is it hard to die? the boy asked Nana, and she looked at him.

She said, What makes you think of that, and he said he didn't know.

She looked down at the board, and then she put her hand on his hand. I don't think so, she said, but nobody's ever come back to tell us, so I guess we really don't know.

But I don't think so, she said. Probably it's like going to sleep. Before you know it, you're sound asleep, and you can hardly remember how you got there.

Mom came in and said, Ready, and he said, Do you mind being the hat?

The hat would be just fine, she said.

She set a glass of ginger ale down for the boy, and a glass of beer for Nana, and then she sat down. She looked over at her son and smiled.

She said, Who's the banker?

Nana said, Who can we trust with all that money?

After he was in bed, the boy thought of Jim on the bottom bunk, sleeping like stone. He thought of Jim dreaming, and he thought of what it would be like to wake up in the morning and find Jim dead. He wondered what his mother and Nana would do, and if they would blame him for not looking after his brother.

He heard Mom and Nana talking, and then he thought of riding his bicycle, and the leaves falling from the trees. He could lean from side to side as he pedaled his bike, and it was almost like drifting in water. Then he thought of the fish in the tanks at Woolworth's, gliding through the rooms of the sunken castle, and darting quickly away from the glass wall of the tank.

Jim turned over in his sleep, and then Nana laughed at something out in the living room.

He thought about the way the man at the church had smiled, and then he thought of the man's sister and brother-in-law and their kids. He yawned, and wondered if the man had found his family.

[23]   Warren

Where is that boy? they said to me. Where did that boy go to, fellow? They wanted to know. I lived over to East Boston then, next to the highway, and the trucks went crash and boom, and the windows, they rattled like bombs were going off outside there. Back then, when that boy went away.

How many years ago was that now, and no boy to show for it. That boy, maybe he went to the moon.

I do not know, I said to them. I do not know. That was not me. I did not take no boy from his mother and also from the home he live in.

That lady. She was a very nice lady, and she saw me and she said, You're a very nice man. You're a handsome man, and you need a little help with the booze, with those mental problems, then you'll be fine forever afterwards. She said, and I fucked that lady real fine, and she had a fine body like silk and something. Then the boy, he came along. Little baby boy, yelled and screamed half the night. Over in Newton. All them rich people in houses with one, two cars.

The boy screamed, and no pills, no nothing for me, so I went out and took a drink. I took a little glass of Carling

Black Label beer, and it tasted fine. Like fucking the lady. So fine.

It loosened me. Me and my troubles, so I tried one more. I said, Okay, and nodded to the man at the bar. One more if you please, and I felt fine all over.

Please, one more, and one more, and on the street later they saw me. I was trying to walk, and I pissed on a parked car.

Two, three guys standing there. They said, You fuck you. You fucking drunk. You got respect for nothing.

Fucking asshole, and one man, he wore a black coat, he hit me in the face. It went crack like a bottle, and one other man, he kicked my balls, and I fell, and they stood and kick my back, my head, my wrist where it was broke.

The lady in Newton, she don't know nothing. She got boy, he was little, and she worked like a dog. Worked her fingers to the bone.

Police say, Who did this, Warren? And I said it was very dark and I had two, three drinks, and I cannot tell to say.

Maybe you can go to meetings, the doctor who set my wrist, he said.

Go to church basement. There were signs, there was coffee and donuts and cookies. You sit on your hands if they're shaking. Smoke cigarettes. Nice man, nice lady. They said, You're welcome to come, Warren. We were like you too once upon a time.

That one drink, the man said. A hospital, a jail cell, an early grave. You drink some more, you take one drink only, that's where you'll go. I speak the truth, the man said.

Sign said, Keep it simple.

Sign said, One day at a time. It said, First things first.

They meant, You drink and you're in big fucking trouble, Warren.

I went over to Everett, I went to South Boston, they take me to Metropolitan State and to Boston State and to Shattuck Hospital, I think.

I had a baloney sandwich. I had coffee and a donut.

They bought me cigarettes. They bought me a carton of Camels, and they said, Here's for you, Warren.

One time the lady came, and she cried for ten and twenty minutes.

What'd you do, Warren honey, she said. You're all broken, and I said, They kicked my balls and punched me in the face. Broke my arm, but back then, I was as strong as a horse or cow.

She did love me many years ago. She had pictures, and she said, That's your boy. He loves you and misses you. Little kid. He ran in diapers, and then they came, the cop came many years later, and said, Where'd this boy go to? You're the father? Where's the boy? Where'd he go off to?

Now the welfare lady, she comes and says, You got food, you got medicine, you got money to support yourself. She's a pretty lady. She's a graduate of Boston College, and she helps with every problem.

In Allston I have a nice room by the trolley tracks. Allston nice, not like East Boston and Everett. It has trees and a nice park.

A man comes in the morning. He says, We all set, Warren. He helps with cooking and with the shower he also helps. Makes bed, washes clothes, does grocery shopping. What do you want, Warren my man? What do you need?

Welfare lady, she says, You watch TV? You like Lady Di and Rose Kennedy and President Kennedy's daughter Caroline? She grew up pretty, and very very rich. She married a man, and she has a baby herself.

So I went to the church basement, and the lady with

the boy, that lady came to visit, and she said, You have a beautiful boy, and he needs you very much, and if you'd take medicine, you'd be A-one, Warren. You'd have no problems with booze, with mental things, no more. No mental, no booze, and everything like morning. The sun, it would be shining, and you'd go to work, and the coffee, it would smell so nice.

She got clean sheets, and she said, Warren, that was a hard time. She said, You're handsome still, my honey, and she put her hand on me and said, Oh Warren, oh Warren, and that was fine.

I could still fuck that lady as fine as ever. She was soft, and she said, Oh, oh, oh, she said, over and over.

Then I sipped more. First the cough syrup. The little boy, the lady, they had colds, they coughed all day and all night. Their throats, their lungs, they went cough and cough.

I took a spoonful, late, when I woke up. The moon was shining, and the heat in the radiator, it moved along in the late night. They all slept. The lady slept, and the boy, he slept too, and baby maybe didn't cry. So I sat on a chair, and I stood up. I looked out window, I could see a streetlight, the cars were all parked. I went to the bathroom. Made water, looked in the mirror.

What're you doing, mister, I said to the mirror. Why aren't you going to sleep?

Then I went to the kitchen, to the cabinet, and found the brown bottle, and it was sticky all over. It was half full, and the spoon, it shook in my hand.

Tasted like cherry, and the next one tasted like cherry and medicine.

So I had that, and felt nice, like fucking the lady, her warm hole, and I found Aqua Velva. That was in the cabinet, in the bathroom.

It didn't taste so good, but I keep it down, and had

some more. I felt pretty good. And that started me off one more time.

The lady cried and said, Now you did it. She said, Why can't you? And why be like this? And you try to kill yourself, and why do this? Your kid. Two kids now.

So they took me, and I do not recall much. It was not me, but a man by the name of Warren. I looked in the mirror, and saw strange eyes, and a person who sleeps in shelters and on the streets.

I got baloney sandwiches, and hot tomato soup, and it wasn't so bad.

I went in, I came out. A tooth fell out, and I cut my foot, and they put me in a white room. It had a mat on the wall and floor, and there was a cage over the light on the ceiling.

Then the policeman, he came and said, You know that boy? He's gone? And where've you been for two, three days?

That boy, I didn't know a thing. I slept, I woke up, I dreamed one or two times. Okay, mister, I said. Okay.

Man, he said. That boy vanished like air. That boy's gone. Nine, ten, that boy. He rode a bicycle, it was locked to a fence, and there's no boy anywhere, anymore.

He's got brown hair, that boy. He's got blue eyes, he's got freckles all over.

Where'd that boy go to, Warren?

The man looked at me. Icy eyes, and I can't tell you, Mister, about that boy. I can't tell you anything.

I don't know him for beans. That lady too. That was so many years ago.

The policeman went away, and that boy, who can tell. He ran to the circus maybe. He ran away to be cowboy.

Who's that boy think he is, leaving like that. He ran away, and the policeman came to me like that. The lady was in Newton. She was a nice lady with two boys, and now it's many years later, and I watch shows on television like that.

They got me a color television. I see *Wheel* and *Most Wanted* and *Unsolved Mysteries*. They're not too smart. Vanna claps, and a man spins. They clap, and it's four hundred dollars, and he won the car, it was brand new. The lights blinked.

The aide man, he comes and he helps me with many fine things. You want ham, you want turkey, you want nice bagels too. Okay, Warren, you tell me and we'll do our best, so you'll have dignity.

That boy, I saw him many years ago. The boy with the lady. He was four, maybe five years old, I think. The lady said, Honey, you come live with your son, and he'll love you very much. Your son needs you. So I loved that boy, and that lady. I washed dishes, cleaned floors. I cooked nice big dinners. The lady worked hard as rocks, and she walked through door very tired at night.

You sit down, I told her. The boy smiled. The boy was missing teeth, and he played with blocks all day.

I fucked that nice lady all night long. She said, oh and oh, and I slid that thing in, out, and she was all wet and silky.

Each night, she said to do that, and she soon got big once more. She cried and said she can't afford it. And the boy played with blocks and said, Daddy, Daddy.

And I said, you be quiet you. What's wrong that you can't keep a quiet mouth.

So I took twenty dollars, and got a pint, and it was very good. It tasted like a pine tree. The hot summer, and I could sleep in the woods, under bushes maybe. I walked two, three miles. The pint was in my pocket like that.

I went to Boston, and sold blood. I got maybe ten more dollars, and they said, Warren, you've been on the street too long. Why don't you be like someone else, they said.

I saw a man, and stayed with the program. I went to meetings and meetings, and drank coffee and ate cookies. Worked construction, and painted houses, and stood on very tall ladders.

Didn't pick up a drink once. Got two months and four months, then maybe one year. Other men, they had one drink, and went to the hospital and jail cell, they went off to that early grave for sure.

I was in a nice room by myself. I had a clean toilet and bathtub, and there were many friends in the program. I went to meetings. I went to Cape Cod, to Dorchester and Wellesley.

I told the story how I drank the cough syrup, and looked in the mirror at a man and said, What are you doing here, mister, and I spit at the mirror, all those many years ago.

Then it was like nothing happened, and I got one nip only, one VO maybe, and I was off and running one more time. In the rooming house, the landlord said, We want rent, old friend, and work wanted to know. You show up there or else. They said you want some help maybe, Warren?

Sometime, I fell on my face and nose, and she hurt like a bastard, and the cut bled all over. The doctor said it didn't look so good. He put me on the sixth floor, so I got good treatment. They showed a movie, how the booze went to the liver and brain and soul.

It's a bad disease. Mental, physical, and in the spirit too. All those parts, they take you down to a bad place, time and again and time and again.

You step on the elevator, and you go down and down. You step off, and that's the end of that.

So I said, Not for me. I didn't know anything at all.

Then later, when they asked about the boy, where he went, and he was only nine, maybe ten. He was in the fourth or fifth grade, and he was a very smart boy too. A very nice boy, and he had a baby brother.

They were worried sick.

I got one pint and one more pint like that. I slept in the cellar, and piled cardboard boxes all over me, and I wasn't too cold like that. I shook all over from toe to head, and then it snowed, and cars went puff on the streets, the cold was below zero.

How come that boy and that lady, they do a thing like that. You watch the boy many many times, and that boy vanished overnight like that.

I have a disease, and it's very hard for me, a very bad time for me. The elevator, they promised it would go down and down, and take me many places I did not think to go. Rats squeaked, and I shook all over, and I saw bad things. They kicked my balls, and there were many cuts and broken bones all over. Doctors all the time, they said give up the drinking, give up that way of life.

Now they give me a very nice life in Allston, on a street with a park. There are many trees and birds, and little kids play.

And the man helps me very much. You want chocolate cake maybe this week, Warren? he says. We get you ginger ale and we get you smokes for after too.

It was very hard for many years. I have no teeth anymore, and my bones ache all over, and scars and tired all the time. I stay on the couch like this, and Welfare, they say you have dignity like that.

The man helps with shaving, and shower, and then medicine too. I have a microwave, I make spaghetti and brownies. It bings at the end, says all done now.

The man and me, we watch *As the World Turns*, *The Young and the Restless*, and see ads for dishwashing liquid and Tuck's Medicated Pads and Pampers, a good diaper. The man helps me with everything. He saves this life for me.

He goes home, and I'm quiet. I hear footsteps in the hall, and watch TV too, and then news and *Wheel* and Vanna, and she's wearing a blue dress, and she's pretty, she claps all the time.

They wanted that boy, and they said, Where's he gone to, Warren, and that was many years ago, and how could I even know. Not me, mister.

[24]   Melissa

He always said, Mom, Mom, Mom, Mom. If I was on the phone, or reading, or trying to do something on the stove, and had to concentrate, he'd stand there and keep saying, Mom, Mom, Mom, Mom, Mom, Mom. He'd say it fifty times if he had to, if he wanted to ask something or tell me something, if he wanted my attention for any of the ten thousand reasons a child needs your attention. Then I would look up, and see him standing there, in the doorway, or at the side of the couch in the living room, and it would hit me all over again that this boy, this kid with the brown hair falling forward and covering his eyes, he was what I had made. And no matter what else or what other things I had ever done or ever would do, no matter about the terrible mistakes I had made, he was there and I had made him as though I was some kind of God or something, and that was worth living a life for, and that made up for anything else, no doubt about it. And I knew that early on, from the moment I was going to have him, and Warren was there. Warren never could have stayed I guess, and been there in any meaningful way. He was just there until the next little thing came along, and I was nineteen, and I thought that all he needed was someone to love him and let him know he was needed, and then when he saw his son I thought he would be transformed by seeing his own flesh, his own breath, in that boy, but that did not happen of course and I will take the blame for that also. I was nineteen, and all the time I kept hoping and believing, and I thought that I would have to have abandoned hope and the capacity to dream before I could give up on Warren, and when he came back, and stayed sober for that year, I really thought it was over, the struggle and the loneliness, and then I had two boys, and he was gone again, and I should have known by then. But what are you going to do. By then it was a fact of my life, and Mom said to me, These two aren't going to go away, so you better buckle down, and I did. And I guess I think of that part of things, of having him, having the first one, and how amazing that is, from the moment you miss your period, and the doctor tells you that yes, you are, and it's still hard to believe because nothing whatever shows. I didn't feel sick at all, and I maybe felt a little tired the first month or two, and I'd wait and wait, and still nothing seemed to be happening, and for a while I thought they had made a mistake, they had mixed up my sample with someone else's. But then my clothes were getting tight, and then I could see and feel the belly, which really wasn't much at first. And Mom was there a lot of the time, and I couldn't have done this without her. I'd wait, and it would be twelve weeks, and then sixteen weeks, and twenty weeks, and even then I didn't have that much of a belly, and people who saw me on the street, I don't think they could tell, not unless they really looked hard, and knew to look.

I won't think of this, because it does no good whatsoever. What was done to him back then would have been such that he could not have lived through it. It does no good, no good to anyone, nor for any purpose, to think and to dwell and to run it through and over and in and out of your mind again and again and again and again, like some terrible broken record that would make you a crazy lady if you had to keep hearing it. So no. Stop. Just stop. Take deep breaths. Take slow deep breaths, and think of Jim, and how he has grown up, and how he comes for dinner, and we sit, and afterward sometimes we watch a movie, and maybe we will mention Mom, and how she is gone seven years already. And what's past is past, and there is nothing I can do, except remember the few years I had him, and what that was like. Because babies do finally arrive. You wait and wait, and then you really show, you feel big as a couch or chair, and there's no mistake, and then you go in the hospital, and one way or another it's coming out, it's going to reach the light of day, and boom, there he was, crying and watching and waving his arms and legs.

I remember the smell of him, because nobody ever mentions that. He smelled like new skin, and powder, and maybe sheets on the line on a windy day. He smelled like a baby, and he would be lying there, after his bath, or after I changed him, and I put my face against his belly or his neck, and I would just breathe, and fill my nose and mouth and lungs with the smell of him, and that was like nothing else.

He would put his fingers in my mouth, and I would pretend to eat his hand or his elbow or knee, would put them in my mouth, and he tasted like baby, he smiled, and laughed to see me with his elbow in my mouth, and he tasted like ten-week baby, like four-month baby, like the best little boy in the world, something smooth and clean and warm.

He had long arms and legs, and pink flesh, and ten fingers and ten toes, and he had fingernails and toenails that were so small and so perfect that I always wondered who could have made them. His eyes were dark at first, were not quite blue to begin with, but then they began to change. They were always large eyes, and they seemed to take in everything, and whenever I walked into the room his eyes would begin to shine with pleasure. And his arms and legs moved almost constantly, seemed to knead, and ride the air like a bicycle, and he could smile, and his face was round, and even then he was a handsome boy.

His skin was flower petals, except when he had a rash, and then it was scaly, the way a reptile must feel. His hair was very thin at first, and felt startlingly soft like his skin. The bottoms of his feet were also soft, but had ridges of skin, and felt like ripples in sand at the beach on certain days. He was dense and surprisingly compact when I picked him up, and he felt perfect when I held him to my chest and neck, warm and solid, and when he nursed, his mouth was powerful; it pulled and sucked at my nipples, and I could feel the milk flowing from my breasts and into him, and that was like nothing anyone could know unless they had done it, to think that he was sucking nourishment from my body, and he would grow bigger and stronger, and I was the earth itself, I was the giver of life.

He gurgled and made bubbles, and he cooed like a pigeon, and he cried in about seventeen different modes. Late at night he cried from hunger, and that was a softer, airier cry, a cry with almost a cough in it. When he was sick he shrieked, when he was bored he bellowed, when he wanted to be picked up he cried nearly the same as when he was hungry, but without the cough. Late at night, especially during the first few months, he snuffled, and moved his arms and legs slightly, and I could always hear him in his bassinet, which was next to my bed, while I was sleeping. It was a mental check every ten or twenty minutes, that he was there, and safe, and that he didn't need anything, not for now, and I would drift down, two or three layers deeper, into sleep.

By one, he was walking, at least a few steps at a time. He was blowing bubbles at the air, and reaching for just about everything, for plates and pillows and blocks and books. He watched me always, and reached for my hands and my hair, and during the time Mom was taking care of him days, I'd come by there after work, tired as a dog, and he would make noises and reach, and I had hours more to go in the day, and it didn't matter because to see him was to remember suddenly why I was doing all this. Warren was off on his thing, and sleeping wherever, and not doing much to help, though once every two or three months an envelope would come in the mail with a dollar or two in it, and sometimes even a five. Maybe that is why I stayed hopeful about him. I thought, If only he could quit the alcohol, then this boy of mine, he would have a father.

Now I live in a town on the North Shore of Boston, about forty miles north of the city. There is a beach, and almost no crime, and in the winter I would say there are no more than four or five thousand people here. I have a one-bedroom apartment, and I am only a five-minute walk from the stores, and from the train station. I go to the bank and the grocery store, to the post office, and I seem to keep busy. Just after Mom died, I thought I had to move away from Newton, and so I came here. Jim can drive up in a little over a half hour, and after dinner and a movie, he will sleep on the couch, and I will hear him during the night. He is thirty-four years old, but hearing him in the living room, the small movement of the covers, or his shifting, I find myself worrying, I find myself getting up from bed, and going to the living room, and watching him. Just standing there near the doorway to the living room and listening as closely as I can to make sure he is breathing.

The nights can sometimes be difficult because I will often think of the past years and how I would sit at the kitchen table in the apartment in Newton. I would sit after he had gone to bed, or later, after they had both gone to bed, and I would drink tea and read, often for an hour or two. We didn't have much of a television then, just an old, half broken one, and I would go to the library once or twice a month, and after they were in bed, and I was sitting at the kitchen table, that was the only time I ever had to myself. And I remember the sounds of the house and street, the quiet sounds there in that humming apartment and suburb and city. A car or a dog or the radiator, or the wall or floor or ceiling creaking, and I would feel happy sometimes just to be sitting there. To have my boys, and a book, and Mom, and to be able to be part of everything. And the thing I remember now is how he would get up from bed, and I would hear him shuffle down the hall, go into the bathroom, not shut the door, tinkle, forget to flush, then he would come and stand in the doorway to the kitchen. His hair matted and sticking up on the side, and his face all puffy with sleep. Wearing those flannel PJ's I used to get for him at King's or Jordan's, with the cars or baseballs or horses on them. He would stand there and just look at me, and not say anything, and I would turn around, and he'd come into my arms. He was always very warm from bed, and I could feel his bones, and smell his hair, and I'd call him my pal, my sweetheart, my best buddy in the world, and he'd finally say, What're you doing? And I'd say, What do you think I'm doing, and he'd say, Reading.

His breath was sour from sleep, and his hair smelled like sleep and shampoo, and he would want to sit down, there at the table, in the yellow light from the lamp on the wall. He'd ask what I was reading, and I'd tell him; usually it was a mystery or sometimes a romance. He'd say, Did you always read, and I nodded. Even when you were a girl? When you were my age? Yes, I'd say, and he'd want to hear about what I used to read when I was seven, or ten, or twelve, and I'd tell him about the Bobbsey Twins or Horatio Alger, which my father had bought used somewhere, or books about traveling around the world or flying an airplane.

How come you didn't have a brother or sister? he wanted to know, and I told him I really didn't know but that maybe because of the Depression, my mother and father didn't want to have more than one kid because they didn't have much money, and sometimes Dad was out of work.

What did he do? Your dad? What'd he do?

I told him that Dad was a carpenter for many years, and that late in the thirties, when I was growing up, he got a job at a factory in Watertown that made washing machines, and he worked there for twenty-seven years, until he retired.

Can I've some milk? he asked, and I said, Sure, and stood up to get him some.

I said, You're just full of questions, and he said he guessed he was, and I said, What about you? Where'd you come from, and how'd you get here, and he looked puzzled. Sweetheart, I said, I'm only kidding, and then he smiled, and finished his milk. He brought his glass to the sink, and rinsed it out, and then he said, Is Warren my father?

He said it like that, I think, and it was one of the last times he came out and talked with me. I think it was September, because school had already started, and I always noticed how tall he was getting, and how blue his eyes were, and I thought that the girls would love him because he was so handsome, and he was such a great kid.

He said, Warren's my father, isn't he? And he had seen his picture, and he seems to have had really misty, faded memories of this man who used to be around, and he must have heard me talk about him to Mom.

I said, Why do you want to know? Even though, looking back, that was a stupid question to ask, because he had every right, every reason on earth to know. But I guess I was stalling for time. This wasn't the first time it had come up, but I had always said, He's sick, or, He's not here, or, He's gone away, but he might come back someday to be with us, to be with you.

This time was different. He was only three months short of his tenth birthday, and that felt like a big thing, and he said, Is Warren my father? and What's he look like? and I said, Why do you want to know? And he said, Because, and I said, Yes, he was, and he loves you very much even though he can't be with you. He has an illness, and he is very very sick, and he goes to the hospital sometimes, and then he stays somewhere in South Boston, and sometimes in Everett, and maybe someday he will come for you, and you will see how much he loves you.

Then I stopped, and he was looking at me, his hair falling forward over his forehead, and he nodded slightly, and looked down, as though that was all there was to it, and I thought, It was that simple and that easy. He just heard it and believed it, because he was a kid and that was what the world was like for him.

And then it was October, and he was nine years old, and he would have been ten in December, a few days before Christmas. It was October, and other than that I don't remember much at all, except that I wanted to scream, but instead I held my breath, and even now to this day I am holding it.

[25]   Medfield State Hospital

Ford lay down on the floor in the back seat of the car, and Henry said, Don't even think of doing anything, and they drove and drove, and the carpet smelled of gasoline and urine and wet soil. He slept for a while, and when he woke up it was dark and they were parked somewhere, at a restaurant on a highway. He could hear traffic, and he sat up for a second, and there were parked cars, and long silver banks of streetlights that bathed everything in pale light. Henry was gone, and Ford could see people leaving the restaurant and walking to their cars, could see people stepping out of their cars, stretching, yawning, patting coat pockets for keys and wallets, checking car doors to see that they were locked.

He curled up on the floor, and waited. He heard voices, and he heard another car come into the parking lot, and he heard a car start up. Then the door opened, and Henry said, You awake. And Ford sat up. Henry patted the seat next to him, and said, Why don't you climb over?

I was nine years old. I was almost ten.

In prison there were steel doors that clanged, and there was a fence that was twenty feet high, that had razor wire on top. Then there was a second high fence, with more razor wire, and a wall beyond that. There were towers at each corner of the buildings, towers with huge glass windows like the windows at airports, and there were two men in each tower, and they had rifles and binoculars.

The halls were long, and echoed, and everything was steel and concrete, and the tiers rose like a wasp's nest. There must have been five or six levels, and there were hands and arms resting on the crossbars, poking through, and there were bells, and buzzers, and someone shouted, Fuck you, somewhere, and there were radios and televisions, and even at night I could hear the men breathing on their bunks, could hear slow echoing footsteps, could breathe the dreams almost, the sweat, the toilets in cells dripping late at night.

The injection is quick. I no longer feel the prick. Just the Prolixin moving into my spine and brain and nervous system. I'm underwater and covered with sheets. They'll bury me. They'll burn my body. The flames will lick at my skin, and all of it will melt away, will flow down like lava.

When do they come? What time?

Five a.m., I think. Long before the sun will rise. They will feed me eggs, toast, sausage, coffee, though I will not feel much like eating. I'll pick, will push the food around on my plate, and two or three of them will be standing outside in the hall.

Already, I will have been moved into a different cell, with no other cells nearby. And they will stand outside, with their keys, their clubs, their mace, and they will say, How you doing there? And I will hand the plate to them. Will say thanks. Will say, All done.

They look at their watches, and sometime after that, the priest comes in. Wearing black, with gray hair, an old red face, blue eyes. He puts his hands on me, on my head and arms and shoulders. He whispers, says, Would you like to make a confession? He takes out holy water, oil, rosary beads, a Missal.

He touches the oil to my forehead and hands, makes small crosses, commends me to God.

The boy was in Illinois, near Chicago. There was a church and a bar, and a granite building for the town hall and police station, and he was only six or seven, had red cheeks, and he said he was waiting for his mommy, but she was late, he thought. Maybe she wasn't coming.

He was in the front seat, and he was very tired, and sometime later, after we crossed into Indiana and then Ohio, he fell asleep, and slumped over, his head against my side.

I drove a long time. I drove through most of Ohio, and Pennsylvania, and into New York State.

Ohio was flat, and there were farms, and I pulled over several times, and Jack and I—his name was Jack—went into a McDonald's, and he wanted a Happy Meal, and he wanted an apple pie, and he wanted quarters for the video games in the lobby outside the bathrooms.

New York State was hilly, and the trees were changing, were yellow and red, and a lot of the time it rained. The sky spit rain, and there was wind that sent the leaves spiraling to the ground.

Jack had a coat and jeans and sneakers, and I bought him a sweatshirt and underwear and chinos at a K-Mart in Ithaca, New York, near a long lake whose water was gray with cold. Then we got a motel room, and I gave him more quarters for the video games, and we ordered pizza.

He took a shower, and put on clean underwear, and I did not touch that boy. He will tell you that.

His name was Jack, and he was from a town near Chicago, and he was seven years old. He wanted a Chicago Bulls hat, and we couldn't find one, so we bought a Buffalo Bills hat instead.

I did not touch that boy. We watched part of a movie on the TV, about a man from the future who comes back to the past to save the world, but we fell asleep halfway through.

He had brown hair, and blue eyes, and he was thin. He cried when we were crossing from New York to Vermont. He said he missed his mommy, and I told him we would call her when we reached Boston. She was probably worrying, I said, but she would be very happy when she heard from him.

And then in Maine, along the coast and near forests that seemed to go on forever, the rain picked up, and seemed to want to wash the world. The windshield swam with water, and sometimes it was hard to see outside.

We crossed into Massachusetts, after passing through a small piece of New Hampshire, near Salisbury, and then went south toward Boston.

It won't take any time at all, they have told me. There will be the waist chain and the shackles and handcuffs, and the sky, in the east, just over the treetops, will be streaked with deep blue and the first wisps of pink.

The table is silver, and I'll lie down, and they'll strap me onto it. Then a doctor will put a needle into a vein in my arm, and at first they will drip Valium into me.

The priest will be there, and a man in a dark suit will read from a paper.

Do you want to say anything? he will ask, and I will shake my head, No.

There will be five people in the room. The man, the doctor, the priest, and two men in white lab coats.

Then I will see the small bottles of clear liquid on a tray.

Steve is off tonight. A man named Archie from E-2 is

working the shift. He is tall and bald, and walks very slowly up and down the hallways. He wears a white shirt and white pants and white sneakers with rubber soles. If it wasn't for the beam of his flashlight, I wouldn't know he was passing.

Henry said you wouldn't know about something unless you were there, and that was important to remember. People didn't understand that.

Then I counted. One, two, three, four, five.

One and one make two.

Two and two make four.

That was a cow. That was a chicken, that was a cat, that was a dog.

The cow says, Moo, the chicken goes, Cluck, cluck, the cat says, Meow, the dog says, Woof, woof.

Be careful, Mom said, and Tate said, Where you going, honey?

In New York City the streets were very quiet at four a.m., and the lights blinked and blinked and blinked. They never stopped.

That was a long time ago. That was almost forever.

What time? What will they say?

We drove down I-93, and off to the left and ahead we could see the lights of the harbor and of downtown. This was late, was almost two a.m., but Jack had slept much of the day and evening, and he was now awake. We crossed over the bridges and ramps, and there wasn't much traffic. Only a few cabs and trucks, a few cars heading home or away to somewhere.

On the Southeast Expressway we went through the center of Boston, past the Downtown, Government Center, and Airport exits, and I saw the sign for the Mass Pike.

90 West, it said.

First we went through a tunnel, then just past the tunnel there was the entrance, and we were heading west, past Copley Square, past Boston University, and I could see the river. We stopped to pay a toll, and I asked Jack how he was feeling.

He said, Okay, and I said pretty soon he could call his mother.

We got off in Newton Corner, which looked different from all those years ago, and we drove along Washington Street. Past Conroy's Funeral Home, past Our Lady's church, and up ahead I could see the Star Market in Newtonville Square.

We went a half mile past the Star. In West Newton I pulled up in front of the police station. There was a blue light out front, and next door was the courthouse.

I told Jack to go in and tell them his name and where he was from, and to say that he wanted to call his mother. Tell them that your friend is outside in the car and that he is waiting. Tell them that he is very tired. They'll know what to do.

He said, Okay, his face calm and serious. Then he opened the door, and got out, and I watched him walk inside.

I shut off the car, and laid my head back against the seat, and waited. I waited a long time, it seemed, but then they were there, were on all sides of the car, and they said, Okay, motherfucker.

Prison was hot and wet, and afterwards, I could go anywhere. There was Florida and Texas. There was Montana, California.

I didn't touch that boy, and that is what he told them. And finally I was in the room in Boston, and there was a hotplate and I drank wine, and someone was pounding on the door.

How long? How many hours and days? How many weeks?

In the name of the Father and the Son, the priest will

say.

On a long hallway lit by bare white bulbs, and the chains will rattle as I move.

The room itself, the chamber, will be painted green, and there will be small windows, with blinds on the outside, and a dozen chairs beyond the blinds.

The door will be like a submarine hatch, with a giant wheel to tighten and seal the chamber. And in the middle there will be a wooden chair, with heavy leather straps to go across my chest and upper arms, my legs, my wrists. The leather will be dark and well-oiled, and it will be dawn, will be five fifty-seven a.m., and they will wear dark clothes, and the priest will make a cross, and I will see them outside in their chairs, on the other side of the blinds.

Then the priest will step outside, and the door will close, and I will hear the wheel tighten. The pellets will fall down a chute and into the solution, and the hissing sound will start, and the smell will be like nothing I have ever known.

She said, Be careful, when she came into my bedroom at night, and she said, You must be very tired, and she said, Did you brush your teeth? Say your prayers?

Our Father who art in heaven, I prayed. Hallowed be Thy name.

She said when she was a girl her mom and dad, they liked to rent a house in the woods in Vermont or Maine, and there was a lake, and she saw a deer, and there were loons, which were birds, and they sounded like owls almost, and she would walk in the woods and imagine that she was another girl in another place, and maybe her real mom and dad were the King and Queen of England, and when she walked out of the woods there would be a glass carriage waiting, drawn by six white horses, and it would take her to a castle on a hill.

Isn't that funny? she said. Isn't that something?

Archie goes by, goes quiet as mice, and there's no moon tonight.

And Henry was sleeping, was snoring slightly, and he had said, You don't know for shit, and he sipped beer, and threw more sticks in the wood stove.

That was a cabin in Oregon, and he swung hard at my head, and I was whirling away, and the side of the table rushed at me, slammed the side of my face, and on the floor everything was buzzing in my head, was hot, and he said, Ellis, loud, and I was spinning away.

Then it was dark and Henry had put a damp cloth on the side of my face, and I was lying on the bed, and he had taken my clothes off, and he was sitting on the side of the bed. He was crying, and he said he was a piece of shit, a worthless piece of shit, and please forgive him, please find it in your heart to forgive him.

His face was wet, and his eyes were white almost, and he said he would never, ever never do that again.

He went away, and later he was lying next to me, and he was stroking the side of my face where it throbbed, and then his hand was on my chest, and he said, Why don't you love Henry? Why don't you love your old pal anymore?

He had taken his clothes off, and he was hard, and he said, Lift your leg, honey, and he rolled me onto my side.

And later he kissed me and said he was very sorry, and he didn't know why it happened that way.

The toilet flushes, and someone walks by in the hall, and it must be three or four a.m. already. Only two hours to go, and they would come in and say, It's time. We're ready.

Okay, mister, the man would say.

The mountains in the distance belonged to God, and the sky was huge, and at night the stars covered the sky like a million Christmas trees. We could drive forever, and we could clean ourselves in the bathrooms at the back of gas stations, and sleepy attendants asked where we were from and where we were headed and how long we'd been on the road.

The boy in the trailer court said he would go to Disney World, and there was a Merle Haggard song on a radio. Next door. Down the hall. A million miles away.

He said they had everything there.

And Marshall was gone. Had smoked all his cigarettes, and got new meds, and he was somewhere else.

Henry pumped gas, picked peaches, loaded boxes, swept floors, cleaned toilets, raked leaves, washed windows, made phone calls, delivered papers—and he did it for me.

He said, Shhh. Just listen, and the woods were full of sounds. Whirrs and clicks and pings.

We would get a place, he said, and a twig snapped, and he whispered, Shhh, and another twig snapped, and we listened. For five minutes, for ten minutes.

He was waiting in the woods, squatting, quiet as a bush or tree. He was smiling and squatting and waiting. His eyes glittered.

They were in Richwood, West Virginia and Meadville, Pennsylvania. On I-35 in Iowa and ALT-27 in Florida.

And all the pretty, dark-eyed children were out there. The children with deep blue eyes, with copper skin, with tiny fingers, and soft, soft hair. And the President smiling and waving, and slumping down, and his son saluted his casket, and he couldn't have been more than three or four.

A boy was up early, was pulling a cart full of newspapers, and his name was Tom, somewhere in California, and it must have been five-thirty. A car pulled up, the driver rolled down the window, and he was lost, he wanted to know the time.

How old are you?

You have a girlfriend?

Wanna see some pictures?

Archie is quiet as air, and they would come for me early, and the room would have a heavy wooden chair, and leather straps, and they would have shaved my head so my hair wouldn't catch on fire. They'd put a kind of jelly on my skin, and then they'd put wires on my legs and arms and a rounded metal plate on my head.

And voices would murmur, and the priest would whisper, Thy kingdom come, Thy will be done, on earth as it is in heaven.

His name was Roger, Carl, Johnny, Will, Bob, Taylor, and he liked baseball.

He liked to watch television.

He liked pizza and root beer, and in the fall he collected chestnuts, and he loved the oily feel of them right after he opened their spiny covers. He kept chestnuts in his top bureau drawer, and Mom said, They are pretty, aren't they.

The boy in Fresno wanted a Snickers, a Coke, a Ring Ding.

The lights of cars passed, and crossed the ceiling and walls. He could sit and be quiet a long time, could sit almost forever, and his mom and dad were dead, and he would be fine. He was really lucky, if he would only stop and think of it.

What would you like to do? Where would you like to go? Tate said, and he didn't know. He couldn't tell her.

And they will pull a lever and the lights will go dim, and my body, my head and arms and thighs, will begin to smoke.

Mom said it was sweet, at first, how I waved at the air, and later she worried because there was never enough money, and she could never really sleep because she wanted to make sure I was breathing.

I rode my bicycle, and the leaves were red, and the fish in the tanks in Woolworth's swam lazily by, and went in and around a sunken castle.

He said, I love you like my own son.

He said, You can do what you damn well please.

You little fuck, he said. You ungrateful little prick.

She said I would sit alone in a sandbox for hour after hour, pouring buckets of sand, making piles, whispering to myself.

It smelled of gasoline in back, and he said, That's it, and he took a pill, and said he could drive a whole week if he had to.

We'll go up the steps slowly, the thirteen steps, and they'll put a black hood over my head. I'll stand on the trap door, and they'll fit the rope around my neck. The drop will snap my neck, and I'll swing and twirl and swing.

The children wore sneakers, they wore nylon jackets, they wore white jeans and blue jeans, red overalls, a girl had a yellow barrette in her black hair, a boy had a Superman tee shirt. They were standing near the restrooms at the state park. They were in a department store. They were in their backyard, and Mom was inside, was upstairs, lying down, because she'd had a headache all morning.

And the man was nice at first. He said his name was Bill. His name was Mr. Jackson, and he was a friend, and he wanted to go for a little ride.

Henry looked over on Friday afternoon in October, and he said, Come on, and I got in. I would have been ten that December.

The blanket itches, but in a few hours they will come and take me to the warehouse near the back gate. There will be a stack of sandbags, and a post and chair in front of the sandbags. They will sit me down, strap me in, pin a red circle over the left side of my chest. Four men with rifles will be standing behind plywood on the far side of the room, and they'll look and aim through a slot in the wood. They'll shoot for the heart.

And the boy on the swings, the boy looking at baseball gloves in the store, the boy on the beach, the one in the backyard—he'll pause, turn, look up. Then it will be over. Silence. Nothing.